42
.75p

G. F. BRADBY

THE
LANCHESTER
TRADITION

John Catt Educational Ltd

First published by Smith Elder & Co in 1914
Republished by The Richards Press in 1954
This edition published in 2003

ISBN: 0 901577 92 8

John Catt Educational Ltd
Great Glemham, Saxmundham, Suffolk IP17 2DH, UK
Tel: 01728 663666 Fax: 01728 663415
E-mail: enquiries@johncatt.co.uk Website: www.johncatt.com
Managing Director: Jonathan Evans – Editor in Chief: Derek Bingham

Printed and bound in Great Britain
by Bell & Bain, Glasgow, Scotland

CONTENTS

INTRODUCTION

This book was first published forty years ago by the now defunct firm of Smith Elder & Co., a few short months before the cataclysm of 1914, and perhaps its excellence was obscured by the graver events which were so soon to follow. It should not have been allowed to remain out of print for so long, and it is now re-issued, without explanation or apology, as one of the best stories of school life ever written.

Godfrey Fox Bradby was the eldest son of Dr. E. H. Bradby, D.D., sometime assistant master at Harrow and Headmaster of Haileybury. "G. F.", as he was known to many generations of schoolboys, went to Rugby and then to Oxford (Balliol) where he gained a first class in Classical Moderations in 1884, a second in Greats in 1886, and a "blue" at Rugger. Going to Rugby as a master in 1888, he became a house-master in 1908, a post which he held until he retired in 1920. He died in 1947 at the age of 84.

So reads a Note printed in the front of the edition published in 1954 by The Richards Press of London.

This edition appears thanks to the efforts of The Rev'd Timothy Hastie-Smith, Headmaster of Dean Close School in Cheltenham, who has obtained the support of the author's descendants.

The Rev'd Septimus Flaggon is said to be based on The Rev'd John Percival, Clifton College's famous founding Headmaster. Starting with 60 boys in 1862, he had built the school up to to 600 boys by the time he left in 1879. Subsequently he became Bishop of Hereford. Although this story is about a school, in essence it is about change and institutional fear of change. As Machiavelli puts it:

'*... There is nothing more difficult to carry out, nor more doubtful of success, nor more dangerous to handle, than to initiate a new order of things. For the reformer has enemies in all those who profit by the old order, and only lukewarm defenders in all those who would profit* *by the new order, this lukewarmness arising partly from fear of their adversaries... and partly from the incredulity of mankind, who do not truly believe in anything new until they have had the actual experience of it.'*

Macchiavelli, *The Prince*

We share, and hope that you will, Mr Hastie-Smith's opinion that it is a superb book, which has never been bettered, and which should be required reading for Heads.

Great Glemham
August 2003

Chapter 1

THE ELECTION

CHILTERN SCHOOL lies just outside the sleepy little town of the same name. Its motto is 'Providendo nec timendo,' and its colours – a happy combination of cerise, orange, and green – are a familiar sight in all parts of the Empire. But the school itself, though second to none in the opinion of Chilternians, who should be the best judges, is not seen so often by the general public as its colours, because it can only be reached by a branch line and the time-table is a difficulty. It owes its inaccessibility to the foresight of its governors who, at the time when railways were invented, succeeded in keeping the main line at a distance; so when the present chairman comes down for Speech-day he generally travels in a motor-car.

Its stone walls are grey with age or green with creepers. Later generations have relieved the monotony by adding blocks of buildings in variegated brick, and nowhere can the genius of Sir George Honeymead, the famous mid-Victorian architect, be studied to greater advantage. But of recent years taste has swung back in favour of uniformity, and, whenever a famous old Chilternian dies – and there are many famous Old Chilternians – an attempt is made to perpetuate his memory by converting the brick into stone. The sick-house, the gymnasium, the workshops, and the lodge have already been transformed; and it is generally understood that, when a certain aged statesman is taken to his rest, the Great Hall will undergo a similar change – unless, indeed, a new chemical laboratory is considered to have prior claims.

The school owes it existence to the generosity of one John Buss, a local farrier, who migrated to London in the early years of the seventeenth century, prospered in his business, and bequeathed a school and a hospital to his native place. Antiquarians have been at pains to prove that what John Buss really did was to endow an ancient but struggling institution that had existed on the same site ever since Benedictine days, and that the history of Chiltern stretches back into the dark ages before even William of Wykeham was born. But the long gap between the suppression of the monasteries and the seventeenth century is hard to bridge satisfactorily, and John Buss is still regarded, officially, as the creator of the famous school. The property which he bequeathed in East London has of late years greatly deteriorated in value, and, when the prior claims of the hospital have been met, the school only nets £92 3s. 11d. per annum out of the endowments. The Liberal papers, however, have not yet discovered this fact, and, when politics are dull, they demand that the revenues of Chiltern shall be restored to the nation and a University for working men built and endowed with the same. This contention helps to keep the memory of John Buss green outside the walls of Chiltern, and there are some who see in him a pioneer of Democracy and a prophet of the University Extension movement. Be that as it may, Chiltern at the present moment is rich, because rich men are content to pay large fees in order that their sons may have the privilege of being educated, exclusively, with the sons of other rich men. The junior masters are of opinion that these large fees should be made still larger, and the salaries of the junior masters raised in proportion; but the senior masters scout this proposal as mercenary. The senior masters at Chiltern are popularly supposed to be better paid than the senior masters at any other school. Whether this is so or not, it is impossible to say for certain; for the senior masters at Chiltern only talk of their salaries to the surveyor of taxes, and, even then, they do so reluctantly.

The town of Chiltern lives to a great extent upon the school, and the authorised tradesmen, who enjoy a practical monopoly, have a lively faith in the value of the goods supplied by them to 'the young gentlemen'; which faith is convincingly reflected in the prices they charge. In the unauthorised trades, that is to say amongst tobacconists and dealers in motor-cycles, air-guns, and translations of the Classics, competition tends to keep prices down. Nevertheless, these illicit traders are always supposed to have done remarkably well in the palmy days of Dr. Gussy.

Notwithstanding this bond of union, there is a traditional feeling of hostility on the part of the town towards the school. This is due, in part, to the fact that the school people are supposed to look down upon the town people, but, still more, to a widely prevalent belief that, somehow or other, the school has defrauded the town of the farrier's benefactions. As this belief is entirely without foundation, it is likely to be lasting.

The country around Chiltern is pretty, if not exciting. There is a round hill (called by the masters 'Soracte,' and by the natives 'the Sow's Back') at a convenient distance from the school, which commands a view over four counties and enables such of the staff as are inclined to obesity to retain a semblance of their youthful shape. In spring the landscape is white with cherry and pear blossom, and in autumn the apples make a cheerful show. There are quiet lanes, peaceful farms, and irritable farmers, who make unreasonable complaints when 'the young gentlemen' break down their hedges, tread down their young wheat, or pillage their orchards.

The climate is of the kind that is commonly called salubrious; for anæmic boys it is generally considered bracing, but it is also recommended as temperate for those who are afflicted with delicate chests. Like all schools in England, public or private, Chiltern stands on gravel, and the drains are of the most approved and up-to-date pattern. Both the gravel and the up-to-dateness of the drains are vouched for by the school porter. The school-rooms are for the most part dark, but of great historic interest, and possessed of an indefinable charm. This charm, and the sense of continuity with a remote past, are generally regarded as an adequate substitute for ventilation. Indeed, many of the senior masters at Chiltern are strongly opposed to ventilation in any form, and prefer their air with a 'bouquet.'

The playing fields, locally known as Colonus, are amongst the noblest in England, and are said to have been the scene of a sanguinary battle between the Danes and the Saxons. The School Antiquarian Society occasionally indulges in feverish bouts of digging, in the hope of unearthing bones or some other memorial of the fray; but, hitherto, they have failed to discover anything but stones and the bowl of a clay pipe. A stream, which flows at the far end of the grounds, provides the schools with a unique swimming-bath (*vide* prospectus). Under Dr. Gussy's thoughtful régime the banks of this stream were planted thickly with rhododendrons and other flowering shrubs, which afford a reasonably secure retreat, on Sundays, for such of the scholars as wish to enjoy a quiet pipe without the fatigue of pedestrian exercise. But etiquette requires that boys who have not yet reached their fourth Term shall smoke elsewhere.

In spite, however, of its ancient school-rooms, noble grounds, and salubrious climate, Chiltern would probably never have become one of *the* public schools of England if it had not been for Dr. Lanchester. When Abraham Lanchester became headmaster, at the end of the eighteenth century, he found the place little more than a county grammar school; he left it an institution of National, almost Imperial, importance.

Chiltern has lived ever since on the memory of Dr. Lanchester. It is natural, therefore, that he should be worshipped as the second and greater founder of the community. John Buss is honoured for his picturesque figure and his priceless gift of antiquity, but Lanchester is the presiding deity. His statue stands in the centre of the great quadrangle, his portrait looks down from the walls of the Great Hall; the library, the workshops, and other lesser buildings, or additions to buildings, are called after his name; and every foreign preacher in the School Chapel, whether he is pleading for peace or war, for Christian unity or Church defence, for social service or Imperial expansion, closes his peroration with an appeal to the memory of Abraham Lanchester. The Lanchester tradition permeates the place like an atmosphere, invisible but stimulating. It is difficult to analyse, for, like all great truths, it states itself in different terms to different minds and has a special message for each. To the general public it stands for the Classics and faith in the educational value of Latin verse. To the masters it means a firm belief in the efficacy of the methods, or absence of method, to which they have become attached through long habit. To the Old Chilternians it embodies the social ideas and customs with which they grew up; and to the boys themselves, if it means anything more than a name, it represents a certain immutability and fixity of things, an as-it-was-in-the-beginning-is-now-and-ever-shall-be attitude towards life that appeals to their best conservative instincts.

THE ELECTION 11

Any change in the hour of a lesson or the colour of a ribbon is regarded as an outrage on the Lanchester tradition, and is popularly supposed to make the dead hero turn in his grave.

In connection with the school tradition it should, perhaps, be mentioned that there is a life of the great man by a friend and contemporary, and that there is nothing in it to suggest that Dr. Lanchester was so acutely sensitive to change. He seems, indeed, to have impressed his biographer as a restless spirit, with new and rather daring ideas about education. Bound in the school colours and stamped with the school crest, this volume is frequently given as a prize, and figures on many a Chiltern bookshelf. But it is seldom read, except by Germans and Non-conformist ministers; for it is ponderously written, and Chiltern is more concerned with the memory than with the life of its great headmaster. In fact, the tradition is an oral rather than a written tradition, and it is perpetually renewed. Chiltern claims to receive a continuous stream of inspiration from its second founder; and the current of the stream runs strongly against change.

But a moment came in the history of the school, when the Lanchester tradition and all that it stands for was threatened with a violent overhauling, if not a complete extinction. After a reign of four-and-twenty years, to all outward appearance peaceful and prosperous, Dr. Gussy suddenly discovered that he had had enough of it and accepted a vacant Deanery. And then the Governing Body, or Council as it is properly called, in one of those fits of absentmindedness to which governing bodies are liable, elected as his successor a comparatively young man of unorthodox views and no practical experience.

The election was one of the seven wonders of the scholastic world. There had been more than a score of candidates for the vacant post, including a successful curate and an unsuccessful army coach; but it was known that only two of them were in the running, Henry Guthridge and the Rev. Ignatius Lawrence. Mr. Guthridge was a layman and an Old Chilternian; he had served an apprenticeship of five years as assistant master at the school, and had since filled the post of Hilbert Professor and Lecturer at Oxford. Dr. Lawrence, a clergyman of advanced Anglican views, hailed from Cambridge, and had won a certain reputation as headmaster of St Cuthbert's, in the north of England. Mr. Guthridge was the official candidate of the staff, and it was believed that he would carry the day, in spite of the Bishop, who was known to be strongly opposed to the appointment of a layman. As for the Rev. Septimus Flaggon, whose name, to everybody's surprise, was added as a third to the select list, nobody treated his claims seriously. Fellow of an obscure college, tutor to a foreign prince, and subsequently president of some educational institution in Wales, his youth and inexperience ruled him out of serious consideration. It transpired, moreover, that he owed his place among the select to some powerful influence in the background. Some said that he was being run by a member of the Royal family; others suspected the Prime Minister; others, again, the Russian Ambassador. But all agreed that he was, where he was, *honoris causa* and as a matter of form. The choice obviously lay between Guthridge and Lawrence, with the odds in favour of Guthridge, in spite of his laymanship.

However, when the Council met at Grandborough, the county town, to come to a decision, it was found that the Bishop had canvassed strongly and that lay and clerical forces were exactly evenly divided. The Chairman of the Council, a man of moderate views, disliked clerical domination, but was also averse from the appointment of an Old Chilternian; so he declined to give a casting vote in favour of either candidate. Neither side would budge an inch, and the contention grew sharp between them. Twice Mr. Guthridge and Dr. Lawrence were called separately from the dingy room in which, together with Mr. Flaggon, they were awaiting their fate, and submitted to a lengthy cross-examination, in the hope that one or other of them would say something to turn the evenly balanced scales. But neither succeeded in detaching the necessary vote.

At length the Chairman, who had a train to catch and a dinner depending on the train, looked at his watch and hinted at an alternative solution. Had the Council sufficiently considered the claims of the third candidate, a man of great promise with very influential backing?

Compromise is an essential feature of the English character, and long hours of enervating discussion, in a stuffy room on a July afternoon, are favourable to its rapid growth. The Council was exhausted, and Mr. Flaggon had some striking testimonials. His orders were a sop to the Bishop, and his reputed unorthodoxy appealed to the lay party. So, at the eleventh hour, Mr. Flaggon was called into the Council Chamber. His appearance was satisfactory, and his answers to a few questions that were put to him by the Chairman and the Bishop gave no offence. He seemed a providential way out of an impossible situation, and withdrew, at the end of the interview, amidst encouraging smiles. Five minutes later, to the chagrin of his rivals and his own surprise, he was invited once more into the Council Chamber and informed that he was headmaster elect of Chiltern. After which the Chairman left hurriedly to catch his train.

At Chiltern the triumph of Guthridge was awaited with quiet confidence. Nobody, except Dr. Gussy, believed that the Council would dare to disregard the explicit wishes of the masters and the personal claims of the only Old Chilternian who was standing – the one man, in fact, who was qualified to carry on, intact, the great Lanchester tradition. So, when the astonishing news came through that Flaggon, and not Guthridge, was the man, it was received at first with blank incredulity, followed immediately afterwards by a burst of passionate resentment. Who was Flaggon, what was Flaggon, who had ever heard or dreamed of Flaggon? The masters were seen talking and gesticulating in excited groups in the great quadrangle.

'It's an insult,' cried Mr. Pounderly, shaking his clenched fist, 'a deliberate insult, aimed at the whole staff. I say a deliberate insult!'

'On the contrary,' said Mr. Bent the cynic (every staff possesses a cynic), 'it's merely another instance of the ironic humour for which the Council is famous.' Mr. Cox, the Nestor of Chiltern, shook his head sadly from side to side with a far-away look in his eyes; Mr. Black, the senior mathematician, was for petitioning the Council, at once, to revoke its decision; and when Mr. Chase, the moderate man (every staff possesses at least one moderate who reads *The Spectator*), expressed a timid hope that the newcomer would be given a fair chance, he was within an ace of being lynched. Even the school porter, a man of solemn demeanour and grave reticence, expressed the opinion that the choice was 'hominous'.

As for Dr. Gussy, who, without committing himself publicly, had worked hard for Dr. Lawrence in private, he was completely prostrated by the blow. Scarcely could he bring himself to make the official announcement to the school in the Great Hall; and, when he did so, it was with the voice and gestures of the Roman praetor announcing after Thrasymene, 'We have lost a great battle.' For several days he affected to regard himself as superseded, set aside, and sulked like Achilles in his tent.

Chapter 2

MR. FLAGGON PAYS A VISIT

THE election of Mr. Flaggon was followed immediately by the resignation of Mr. Cox. Mr. Cox was in the habit of resigning whenever his proposals were voted down or his advice neglected. Dr. Gussy had, at various times, received twelve such communications from him and, on each occasion had found no difficulty in persuading Mr. Cox to reconsider his decision. There is every reason to suppose that Mr. Cox expected a similar issue to his thirteenth act of protest. But he had chosen his time badly. Dr. Gussy merely said, '*I* no longer count,' and forwarded the letter to the headmaster elect. And the headmaster elect, unfamiliar with Mr. Cox's idiosyncrasies and much impressed by his age, which was seventy-five, accepted the resignation in a courteous and gracious spirit.

Mr. Cox had so long regarded himself as an integral and necessary part of Chiltern and the Lanchester tradition that he was mortified to find how calmly his departure was taken. His colleagues, indeed, were most sympathetic, and said that his going would be a terrible break with the past, and that they would miss him increasingly. But they added that they thought he had acted very wisely in choosing this particular moment to leave them; and this was not the sort of consolation that Mr. Cox expected or desired. It is said that he still regards himself as the first and most notable victim of the new régime, and speaks contemptuously of 'poor old Gussy, who couldn't play a winning hand even when he held all the trumps.' How exactly the hand *should* have been played is not clear; but the implication is that Mr. Cox's resignation was the ace of trumps, and that, rightly used, it would have brought the Council to its senses and prevented untold calamities.

But, if Mr. Cox's resignation was taken calmly, Mr. Flaggon's appointment continued to stir Chiltern to its lowest depths. Articles were disinterred from the back numbers of magazines, educational or otherwise, in which Mr. Flaggon had spoken slightingly of the public schools and public school methods; and the press was deplorable. The Liberal dailies hailed the appointment as the beginning of a new era and the death-blow to an antiquated tradition. Even a leading Conservative journal, which should have known better, described the election as a daring but interesting experiment, and proceeded to sketch an ideal curriculum, for the benefit of the new headmaster, in which Greek was abolished and its place taken by compulsory military drill. The Council blushed uneasily at finding itself suddenly in the van of progress, and began to say harsh things about its Chairman; and its Chairman was only partially comforted by an assurance from the distinguished person behind the scenes that they had chosen the best man in, 'a man who will think before he acts and who will go far.' For to the Chairman the ideal headmaster was rather a man who would mark time decorously than an explorer of untrodden ways.

To the masters the suggestion that Chiltern needed reforming – 'turning inside out,' they called it – was, to say the least, unpalatable. As practical men they despised the theorist; and, of all forms of theorist, the one that they most disliked was the educational enthusiast – the innovator, the impostor. Mr. Pounderly went about with a scared face and mysterious air, whispering 'lamentable, lamentable' to his colleagues; and Mr. Woburn, the scientist, who affected metaphors and frequently mixed them, declared that, though the Classics were undoubtedly overdone at Chiltern, he hated the idea of a man who would always be trying experiments and pulling them up by the roots to see how they were shaping.

The idea of petitioning the Council against the appointment had been abandoned, partly on the advice of the moderates, but chiefly for lack of support from the juniors. For, on second thoughts, the juniors discovered that they did not want the new headmaster to be a nominee and creature of the veterans. The senior masters at Chiltern were famous for their longevity and for the tenacious way in which they clung to the posts of vantage; and, if change meant only a gradual shifting of the senior masters, there was something to be said in favour of change. But it was clearly understood that if Mr. Flaggon attempted to drive his staff along new and unfamiliar ways, he would find them a most awkward and intractable team to handle.

Amid the babel of tongues there was one man who maintained what was, for him, an attitude of unusual reserve. This was Mr. Chowdler, the strong man of Chiltern. Mr. Chowdler owed his reputation for strength, not to any breadth of view or depth of sympathetic insight, but to a sublime unconsciousness of his own limitations. Narrow but concentrated, with an aggressive will and a brusque intolerance of all who differed from him, he was a fighter who loved fighting for its own sake and who triumphed through the sheer exhaustion of his enemies; and a Term in which he did not engage in at least one mortal combat was to him a blank Term. A tall man, with broad shoulders, round head, thin sandy hair, and full lips, he caught the eye in whatever company he might be, and his resonant voice arrested attention. At golfing centres, in the holidays, he was not always a very popular figure. But his confident manner impressed parents, and his was considered *the* house at Chiltern. People often wondered why he had never stood for headmasterships or sought a wider scope for the exercise of power. In reality he had never felt the need. He had so completely identified himself with Chiltern that it never even occurred to him to leave it; and his had for many years been the master mind that shaped the destinies of the school.

In saying this we are not forgetting the existence of Dr. Gussy. But Dr. Gussy, though he had been the titular chief for nearly a quarter of a century, had long ceased to be the ruling spirit. In vulgar phrase, he had allowed Mr. Chowdler to 'run him', and it was generally supposed to be weariness of bondage rather than of power which had induced him to resign before the completion of his twenty-fifth year of office. In appearance he was a complete contrast to his formidable lieutenant. Small and rather fragile, with silver-white hair and a refined, delicately moulded face that suggested Dresden china, he was the type of the old-fashioned scholar. Though there was nothing commanding in his personality, it was none the less distinguished, and the thinness of a high-pitched, and sometimes almost squeaky, voice was atoned for by the perfection of his articulation. In his younger days he had taken a prominent place among the champions of the Oxford Movement, and if he had not become a headmaster, he might have been notorious as a theologian; indeed, his commentary on the Epistle of St. Clement is admitted by all to be a remarkable work. Fathers of Chiltern boys loved to hear him read the lessons, and mothers frequently remarked, 'What a lovely face!' But he was by nature too refined and sensitive to cope successfully with the robust methods of Mr. Chowdler, and, after struggling fitfully for some years, he had purchased comparative peace by an irritable submission. Mrs. Chowdler, an obtuse little woman who worshipped her husband and imagined that everybody at Chiltern shared her admiration, used to say that 'Harry' was the headmaster's better self. She had herself always been ready and willing to be a sister to Mrs. Gussy; but after a long series of pointed rebuffs, she had abandoned the attempt, and the relations between the two families were official rather than cordial.

It was not likely that Mr. Chowdler would approve of the new appointment; indeed, he seldom approved of any arrangement that was not of his own making. But his attitude was one of amused banter rather than of fierce hostility, and he spoke with a good-natured smile of the 'Empty Flaggon.' 'Wait and see' was his advice. 'You will find that the place and its traditions are too strong for the empty one. He may froth and he may fume, but he can't hurt *us*. We are strong enough to assimilate a whole cellarful of Flaggons.'

These and similar remarks made it clear to the initiated that Mr. Chowdler proposed to run the new headmaster, as he had run his predecessor.

In the middle of July Mr. Flaggon paid his first visit to Chiltern. The position of a headmaster elect is a delicate one, and he wisely declined to be introduced formally to the school. If omens count for anything, the circumstances of this visit were inauspicious; for it coincided with a period of four-and-twenty hours of continuous rain. Mr. Flaggon carried away a general impression of gloom and dripping umbrellas; but one incident, trivial in itself, left a permanent record on his memory. During one of the brief pauses in the downpour, he was walking with Dr. Gussy across Colonus towards the Lanchester workshops, and on the way met three of the bigger boys who were sauntering slowly in the opposite direction. There was something about their gait and manner which, if not exactly insolent, at least suggested a complete absence of anything like awe in the presence of their headmaster. They gave a perfunctory salute; and before they passed out of earshot, a voice, which made no attempt to lower itself, remarked:

'Is that the new Gus?'

'Looks like it,' replied a second voice, in the same devil-take-me-if-*I*-care tone, 'unless it's his shuvver.'

Mr. Flaggon, who with the principles of a democrat combined all the instincts of a despot, lifted his eyebrows in surprise and his fingers tightened unconsciously round the handle of his umbrella. But Dr. Gussy appeared to be quite unconcerned and made no comment.

Under the depressing climatic conditions the hours passed rather slowly. Dr. Gussy was courtesy itself, but he found it impossible to be cordial or communicative to a man who was the last person he would have chosen as his successor; and Mr. Flaggon felt it a relief when Mrs. Gussy carried him off to inspect the house and talk fixtures. Dr. Gussy had wisely left all the business arrangements in the hands of his wife, a capable woman with all the capable woman's contempt for the supposed ignorance of a young man and a bachelor; and it soon became evident that Mrs. Gussy intended to take full advantage of her superior knowledge. With a happy mixture of adroitness and authority she forced upon the incoming tenant the oldest carpets and the least successful bits of furniture; and, with equal skill, she secured a tacit permission to carry off some of the more desirable fixtures.

'We are taking the tiles with us to the Deanery,' she would say, pointing to a fireplace; 'but, of course, we shall leave you the linoleum and that very useful deal cupboard. They were both made for the room.'

Mr. Flaggon had no desire to haggle, but he had the Northerner's dislike of being done; and, before the round was over, he found himself in revolt. Mrs. Gussy described him afterwards as 'close'; and Mr. Flaggon, in relating his experiences to his mother, said that if Mrs. Gussy had been a little less autocratic, she would have made an excellent sales-woman. The youngest Miss Gussy, a girl of seventeen and the only other member of the family who was at home did not put in an appearance. She could not bring herself to shake hands with the supplanter of her father, the 'horrid man' who was going to live in *their* house and enjoy *their* garden. If Mr. Flaggon had been an angel from Heaven, she would have hated him with equal fervour. So she withdrew for the day to the Pounderly's and contented herself with a glimpse of 'the man' from a window; which glimpse confirmed her in her worst forebodings. Mrs. Chowdler, who had a talent for saying the wrong thing, remarked that it would be 'a very happy coincidence' if Mr. Flaggon and Miss Gussy took a fancy to each other, as it would give a continuity to life at Chiltern and make the impending change 'so much less felt'. With the object of promoting such a match she spoke warmly to the youngest Miss Gussy of the new headmaster's personal appearance, and was dismayed at the violent outburst which her eulogy provoked.

In the evening, after dinner, Mr. Chowdler called by arrangement and carried off his new chief, nominally to introduce him over a quiet pipe to a few colleagues, but really to take his measure and begin the training of which he was supposed to be in need.

Mr. Flaggon did not smoke, neither did he drink; but he was placed in the easiest of the study chairs, next to the fireplace, and the colleagues lit their pipes and arranged themselves in a semi-circle round the empty grate. There is always something singularly dispiriting about an empty grate on a wet summer evening, and a semi-circular formation round it emphasises its forlornness. The colleagues were conscious of a feeling of constraint. After all that they had been saying and thinking about him in the past week, they were shy of being over-cordial to their new chief, and some of them felt a little as if they were taking part in a conspiracy, engineered by Chowdler, to exploit the inexperience of the new man.

Mr. Flaggon, for his part, did not possess the easy manner and command of small talk which put strangers at their ease. Though anxious to be friendly, he was by nature reticent, one of those who, in new surroundings, are more disposed to receive impressions than to create them. So, after a little desultory talk about the golf links, and several ineffective openings that led into blind alleys, the conversation suddenly expired, and the colleagues found themselves gazing desperately at three iron bars and some unhealthy-looking green and yellow paper behind them.

This was the psychological moment for Mr. Chowdler. Hitherto he had been busy pouring out whisky-and-sodas and struggling with a refractory pipe; but he now sat down opposite the guest of the evening and opened the main attack.

'I suppose,' he began, 'that you have been hearing a good deal to-day about our great headmaster, Dr. Lanchester. Have you ever studied his life?'

'I have indeed' replied Mr. Flaggon; 'in fact, it was one of the first books that excited my interest in public school education. It might, no doubt, have been better written; but it is, in its way, I think, one of the most suggestive books in the English language.'

'Oh, I'm so glad to hear you say that!' cried Mr. Chowdler. 'I'm so glad to hear you say that; because, you know, we cling very, *very* faithfully here to our past and our great Conservative tradition.'

'Aren't you forgetting,' said Mr. Flaggon quickly, 'that Dr. Lanchester was always considered a Radical?'

Mr. Chowdler *had* forgotten; all Chiltern was in the habit of forgetting this unpleasant fact. But he would not own to any lapse of memory, and his voice took on a note of challenge as he replied:

'Oh, a name doesn't frighten *me*; there's nothing in a name; names are only the coinage of the foolish. Lanchester was a man of very conservative instincts. He was not one of those who love change for change's sake. He was a restorer, not a destroyer.'

'It must be difficult to be the one without the other,' remarked Mr. Flaggon quietly; 'and I have always heard that Dr. Lanchester was both.'

Antipathies are often physical as well as moral, and the two men suddenly became conscious of a kind of physical distaste for one another. In Chowdler's fleshy limbs, broad shoulders, bullet head, and aggressive manner, Mr. Flaggon saw for a moment the personification of that narrow but confident prejudice which blocks progress and strangles reform; while Mr. Chowdler realised acutely that 'the man Flaggon' would easily get on his nerves. There was an awkward pause which Mr. Beadle filled by remarking:

'You must have found it very interesting work tutoring a foreign prince.'

But Mr. Chowdler, though momentarily disconcerted, was not to be diverted from his main purpose; and, before Mr. Flaggon could frame a reply, he interposed again.

'Talking of princes reminds me of something that happened to me a little while ago.'

Mr. Chowdler had a large stock of anecdotes with which his colleagues were painfully familiar, for he was never afraid of repeating himself. In theory Mr. Chowdler scorned sentimentality and even sentiment, but in practice his stories were nearly all of the sentimental order and related how small boys had looked up at him wistfully, or old boys had grasped his hand with manly tears in their eyes. And both wistful small boys and manly old boys had nearly always contrived to say something illuminating about the Lanchester tradition.

When once Mr. Chowdler was started, he passed from one story to another without a halt. Mr. Flaggon was conscious that the anecdotes were being related not *to* him but *at* him. However, he smiled when a smile seemed to be expected, and looked impressed where it was obviously the right thing to look impressed. But, when his host concluded the fifteenth story with the remark, 'And I think it's such a splendid idea that the old traditions are being planted, with the old flag, far away over the water, in Saskatchewan,' he could not help saying:

'Don't you think it would be better, perhaps, if the Colonies were allowed to create their own traditions and their own ideals? If there is to

be development, there must be new forms; and I always hope that the
Colonies will have something new to teach *us* some day.'

Mr. Chowdler did not agree, and he said so in words which produced
another awkward pause; and Mr. Beadle once more came to the rescue by
remarking:

'I suppose they are very keen about education in Wales?', which
showed that Mr. Beadle had been making a study of the new
headmaster's previous history.

When the marble clock on the mantelpiece pointed to eleven, Mr.
Flaggon rose to go. A day with Dr. Gussy, and an evening spent in the
company of Mr. Chowdler, had induced an unusual feeling of
weariness. He and his host shook hands at parting with every outward
appearance of friendliness; but, as he walked home under the dripping
trees to the Prætorium, as Dr. Gussy's house was called, he was
conscious that, amongst the many problems that he would have to face
at Chiltern, Mr. Chowdler would almost certainly be one of the most
difficult.

Chapter 3

EXIT DR. GUSSY

THE last fortnight of the term was largely devoted to saying good-bye to
Dr. Gussy. It was traditional at Chiltern for a headmaster to be received
with curses and dismissed with blessings; and an unwritten law required
that, as his last term drew to a close, words of ill-omen should become
few and fewer. During the last fortnight, even Mr. Chowdler gave up
speaking of 'silly old Fussy' and substituted 'poor old Gussy,' or, more
rarely, '*dear* old Gussy.'

Dr. Gussy had never identified himself very closely with the life of
the school, nor allowed himself to become absorbed in its daily
happenings; his youngest daughter probably knew far more about the

inner life of Chiltern than he did, and could address by their nicknames boys of whom her father had some difficulty in recalling the surname. Outside interests had taken him frequently from Chiltern and the branch line (like all branch lines) made it easier to leave Chiltern than to get back to it. He had often missed important matches, his place had frequently been empty at Sunday chapels, and he had been known to confuse the identity of important people. A current story, of which there were many variations, made him address the senior fag of Mr. Cox's house as the junior master on the staff. But his rule was mild and his nature unsuspicious; so he had always enjoyed a fair measure of popularity, and, during his last fortnight, he was positively worshipped.

Dr. Gussy himself was quite unconscious of any sins of omission. He was fond of boasting that Chiltern was a school that 'ran itself'; and, as a proof of its good discipline and high moral tone, he would say proudly, 'For the last seven years I haven't had to expel a single boy – not a single boy.'

This record greatly impressed anxious parents, and had attracted to the school several sons of the titled plutocracy, whose sensitive natures required considerate and tactful handling rather than the rough and ready methods in vogue elsewhere. Dr. Gussy was proud of the distinguished names that figured on his school lists, and never had Chiltern been more popular or more prosperous than during the last seven years of his reign.

Needless to say, the Doctor received an incredible number of presents. It was like a second wedding. Each division of the school gave its separate gift, and, at the earnest request of Mrs. Gussy, who valued spontaneity above all things, the boys were left to make their own choice without prompting from their elders. The Lower School gave a tantalus, big enough to blast the reputation of the most saintly Dean; the Removes, a telescope of immense power, because, in Dr. Gussy's sermons, there were frequent allusions to the stars; the Fifths, an invalid's chair of elaborate mechanical cunning, and the Prefects a complete set of engravings of Chiltern from its earliest days, of which Dr. Gussy already had duplicates in a portfolio. Only the Old Boys, instead of giving anything to Dr. Gussy personally, presented his picture to the library (none might hang in the Great Hall save Dr. Lanchester only), and by a happy thought, entrusted the painting of it to an Old Chilternian whom Nature had intended for a caricaturist, but who had elected to win fame as a portrait-painter.

And to each division separately Dr. Gussy made one of the felicitous little speeches for which he was famous. To the Lower School he said that, whenever he saw that splendid tantalus on his sideboard, for he should give it the place of honour on his sideboard (those who knew Mrs. Gussy best thought otherwise), he should remember the kind thought of the givers and be with them again in the spirit. (Cheers, but no laughter, the Lower School being in too solemn a mood to anticipate a jest.) To the Removes he said that he would now be able, from his peaceful Deanery, to watch the Removes, through his telescope, studying their lessons with the zeal and enthusiasm for which they had always been famous. (Laughter and applause.) To the Fifths he said that whenever he reclined in that luxurious chair – and he hoped that he would have time and leisure at last to recline, occasionally, in an easy-chair (suppressed amusement), he should always think of the happy, strenuous days which he had lived amongst them and for them; for they had always been, and always would be, very near to his heart. (Emotion, and a murmur at the back of 'Good old Gussy.') To the Prefects he said that, whenever he looked at those beautiful and interesting prints – and he should look at them daily, for they would be hanging on his walls (cheers) – he would see the dear old place re-peopled again with the faces that he had now before him, and take courage in the thought of the simple, manly, unostentatious, but whole-hearted devotion to duty which had always been characteristic of the Prefects at Chiltern, and which had given its high moral tone to the school that they loved so well. (Prolonged sensation.)

But it is unnecessary to quote further. It is enough to say that there was a general atmosphere of mutual good-will and esteem, in which impositions were daily remitted (except by Mr. Black, who lacked imagination), and everybody felt that he was an integral part of a great institution, bound by ties of personal devotion to the headmaster, and doing yeoman's work.

One of the most successful functions of this epoch was the farewell dinner, given by the junior masters in Common Room to their chief. Though the masters at Chiltern lived in lodgings or in private houses of their own, it was part of the Lanchester tradition that the bachelors amongst them should dine together once a week in Common Room. A spinster lady, distantly connected with the school, had bequeathed funds for this purpose; and, though the cooking was not recherché nor the conversation of much general interest, the weekly dinner was valued as a picturesque ceremony in keeping with the atmosphere of the place, and was hedged in with a rigorous etiquette. Thus, when any member of the community succumbed to matrimony, he was expelled with a quaint and time-honoured ritual. Some awkwardness had arisen when Mr. Flyte, after being formally 'inhibited' from 'bread, beef, and trencher,' was thrown over by his fiancée at the eleventh hour; for the inhibition had always been regarded as final and irrevocable, and there was no precedent to serve as a guide. Mr. Flyte, however, solved the difficulty with great tact, by never applying for re-admission as a bachelor and allowing himself to be reckoned, for dining purposes, as an honorary widower.

But though the etiquette was formal and the Common Room dinner sacred to bachelors, it was decided, unanimously, that a point might be stretched in favour of a departing chief. Dr. Gussy was invited and Dr. Gussy accepted.

The preparations were on an unusual scale and were in the hands of Mr. Rankin, who was good at that kind of thing and proud of his *savoir faire*. An ice-pudding was ordered from Smith's, the school confectioner; the library attendant and the under ground-man, who waited, were put into dress clothes for the occasion; and Mr. Grady's sister kindly arranged the flowers. Mr. Chase, the senior member and president, provided a special brand of champagne from his private cellars, and there were three savouries and no less than six liqueurs. Dr. Gussy was placed at the head of the table, with Mr. Chase on his right and the newest appointment to the school on his left. Dr. Gussy was but little known personally to the younger members of his staff, and his conduct had not always escaped criticism; for, when he had been suffering much at the hands of Mr. Chowdler, he was in the habit, to use a vulgar phrase, of 'taking it out of' the juniors whom he did not fear. But on this occasion, he was not only courteous, but anecdotal and intimate. For the first time, Dr. Gussy and his junior masters discovered each other; and the discovery only added to the pain of separation. The party broke up at a late hour and everybody went home murmuring 'dear old Gussy'; except, of course, dear old Gussy himself, who had been plied generously with the ice-pudding and the six liqueurs, and who, after a restless night, woke up the next morning with something of a liver.

On the last night but two of term there was another and a more questionable display of feeling. At the witching hour of eleven p.m. a considerable portion of the school (estimates of the exact numbers varied) picturesquely clad in bed-clothes and pyjamas, and armed with sackbuts, psalteries, dulcimers and all kinds of music, appeared suddenly on the headmaster's front lawn and proceeded to serenade their chief with a topical song, of which the chorus ran as follows:

'Young sir, do not answer at random,
No boy should be seen on a tandem.'
Oh, whatever we think of the Badger or Mink,*
De Gussibus non disputandum.

A remnant of sanity kept the headmaster from appearing in person, but his wife and the youngest Miss Gussy, who were not insensible to such attentions, showed themselves at the open windows of the drawing-room and were acclaimed uproariously – especially the youngest Miss Gussy.

It was felt, however, amongst the staff, that things were going a little father than was wise. Loyalty is all very well, but loyalty should be tempered by discretion; and the house-masters came in for some criticism on account of their supposed connivance. Even Mr. Plummer, the most

* The Badger = Mr Bent; the Mink = Mr Grady.

confirmed of optimists, had misgivings and observed next day in Common Room:

'It really does look as if some of the house-masters had been a little slack; unless, of course, the whole thing has been very much exaggerated.'

'It has, as you say,' replied Mr. Bent, 'been very much exaggerated. There were, in reality, no boys, no music, no song, no Miss Gussy. The whole thing was a phantasm of the living, an allegory, an unsubstantial pageant that fades and leaves not a wrack behind. I know it for a fact.

'What do you mean?' asked Mr. Plummer.

'I have questioned each of the house-masters separately,' replied Mr. Bent, 'and each has assured me, in tones of the deepest conviction, that his own Prefects can be trusted absolutely, and that it is, moreover, physically and structurally impossible for any boy to leave that particular house after dark without the knowledge of his house-master. Each has further informed me that, if only the other house-masters would take the same simple and commonsense precautions, such scenes as the one we are deploring to-day would be impossible. Now, what do you say to that, Plummer? You are surely not such a cynic as to doubt the word of a house-master?'

Mr. Chowdler treated the matter in a more serious spirit. He had watched the unexpected apotheosis of Dr. Gussy without enthusiasm – 'sentiment run mad' he called it – and the official countenance given to the serenade by Mrs. and Miss Gussy filled him with indignation. He felt that it was high time for somebody to speak to the 'silly old man.' When duty called, Mr. Chowdler was not the man to shirk an unpleasant task, and his sense of duty was sharpened by a strong personal dislike of Mrs. and the youngest Miss Gussy. He therefore appeared in the headmaster's study after lunch, wearing the particular expression which Dr. Gussy had learned to associate with some of the unpleasanter moments of his own life.

Now, Dr. Gussy had been as much surprised as anybody at the sudden blaze of popularity of which he had been the centre; but, being naïve and not addicted to self-analysis, he had thoroughly enjoyed it. Moreover, the days of his bondage were almost accomplished, and he no longer felt afraid of any man. So he did what he had not done for many a long day,

namely, snapped his fingers in Mr. Chowdler's face, and even told him
not to be an old woman – at least, so Mrs. Gussy told her friends, and a
Dean's wife must be supposed to speak the truth.

Mr. Chowdler gave a somewhat different version of the encounter, in
which the honours were made to rest with himself rather than with his
chief. But even he could not conceal the fact that he had received a
diplomatic rebuff. He relieved his feelings by calling together his house
Prefects and giving them one of his straight manly talks. 'Things,' he
said, 'are shaky – you would probably call them "dicky"; but I call them
shaky – and with anxious times ahead of us next term, we can't afford to
be playing ducks and drakes with our best traditions; and, what with
weakness at the top and giddy heads at the bottom, that's just what some
folks are beginning to do. You know what I am referring to – that
ridiculous scene last night. I know what you think about it. You and I
understand each other, and we know where the blame lies. We needn't dot
the i's, but there are certain houses, not a hundred miles from here, which
would be better for a taste of our friend Archie's strong arm.' Here 'our
friend Archie,' who was head of the eleven, fidgeted uncomfortably.
'Now, I want you to remember,' continued Mr. Chowdler impressively,
'that your influence ought not to end with the house. I want you to talk
sense to giddy heads and to strengthen feeble knees. I want you to set
your candles on a hill where the whole school can see them. I want you,
when everybody else is failing, to be the pillars and the props of our
grand old Lanchester tradition.'

The Prefects in Mr. Chowdler's house were genuinely afraid of Mr.
Chowdler, though they had long learned how to manage him. They now
looked portentously solemn, confessed that they had heard rumours of
the impending 'rag' beforehand, but had not taken them seriously, and
admitted that Mr. Cox's house was not as good as it had once been. But
they were much too tactful and considerate to let out that, as holders of
the cricket trophy, they had themselves headed the procession in a body.

The upshot of it all was that people were just a little anxious as to what
might happen at the school concert on the last night of term. Even Dr.
Gussy confessed privately that he would be glad when the concert was

over. For a great many Old Chilternians were expected for the occasion,
and, when Old Boys get together and become excited, they are sometimes
– not rowdy, of course, but, perhaps, a little boisterous; and then the
school catches the excitement and loses its sense of proportion. Still, the
boys at Chiltern were all gentlemen; and, if you treat gentlemen *as*
gentlemen, they may be trusted to behave as gentlemen. Everybody at
Chiltern believed that, except, perhaps, Mr. Bent, who was a cynic and
believed nothing, and Mr. Grady, the science master, whose face always
had a hunted expression and who sometimes came out of school with
mice in his pockets and his hair full of flour.

However, in spite of forebodings, the concert was not much more noisy
than concerts usually were at Chiltern. Dr. Gussy was cheered to the
echo, and, though he had taken his official farewell of the school only
half an hour before, he was obliged to come on to the platform and make
another speech. Mrs. Gussy smiled her acknowledgements from her
place, and the youngest Miss Gussy was in tears. As for the school song,
it went with a roar that nearly lifted the roof off the Great Hall. The song
of Chiltern is not essentially different from other school songs. Without
ever lapsing into poetry, it maintains, throughout, a fair rhythm and a high
level of imbecility. Its opening verse has served as a model to many
imitations:

> John Buss was a farrier bold,
> And he turned his sweat into drops of gold;
> He fought hard battles, and when he died
> He left a school for his country's pride,
> The best of schools, that has won renown
> From Chiltern chimes to the frontier town.

Chorus: John Buss, John of Us,
> Played good cricket and made no fuss.

To realise the full possibilities of the song, you must go to Chiltern and
hear it sung: especially the chorus, where, after the trebles have piped

'John Buss,' the whole school joins in with 'John of Us.' The effect is electrical and intensely moving.

When the concert was over, the Old Chilternians played a game of football in Colonus by moonlight, and afterwards paraded the town, arm in arm, singing school songs. There were more than a hundred of them, and they sang in different keys; so that the townspeople did not have a very tranquil night.

And in the second week of the holidays, when everybody had gone away and the whole place was in confusion, Mr. Flaggon came down unexpectedly, and insisted on making a more detailed inspection of the school than had been possible during his first visit; much to the annoyance of the porter, whose mind was not as clear on that day as he could have wished, though his face was more solemn than ever. Amongst the buildings visited was Mr. Cox's old house, which was undergoing extensive repairs for its new proprietor, Mr. Chase; and there, on certain walls, Mr. Flaggon found writing which, though he did not fully understand it, made him glad that he had accepted Mr. Cox's resignation.

Chapter 4

THE FIRST SKIRMISH

MR. FLAGGON had come to Chiltern with a determination to do great things for education. He himself had had a hard struggle to win to knowledge, and the phases of the struggle had left their mark deeply imprinted on his character. Born with a thirst for knowledge, he had had to force his way, step by step, to the fountain-head; and the narrow circumstances of a Cumberland vicarage has strewn the path with difficulties. Old and musty books spelled out by candle-light in his father's study, then a scholarship at a decaying provincial grammar school, and finally a classical exhibition at a small Oxford College – such had been the stages by which he had made his way up the stream. And, when he reviewed the past, he could not but remember how brackish and unsatisfying the water had often been in the channels where he had been compelled to seek it. If his thirst had been less insatiable, his own experiences might well have cured him of the desire to drink.

To a childhood spent among the Cumbrian Fells he owed a robust constitution and a toughness of fibre that defied fatigue; perhaps, too, a certain gravity and reticence which seem to come naturally to those who are bred among mountains. Rather below middle height, with a clear-cut face and an intellectual forehead, his most striking feature was his eyes – fearless, grey, receptive eyes, which looked out upon the world with a quiet but penetrating interest. A friend, who knew him intimately, described them as seeing, rather than speaking, eyes.

Of public schools he knew nothing from the inside, and he had few opportunities of studying public school men at his own small college. In such as he came across he had noted a certain self-sufficiency and polite lack of interest in things intellectual, which he put down to the narrowness of their training. The circumstances of his own upbringing had thrown him almost entirely among boys and men who had to make their own way in the world, and who were desperately intent on turning even half a talent to profitable use. Their aims might be low and their ambitions sordid, but there was no trifling with opportunity, no deliberate rejection of golden chances. He had had no practical experience of that large and wealthy class of people who had been well off for two generations and whose children are born with an assured future – the people, in fact, who send their boys to the richer public schools; and he had yet to learn how paralysing to the intellectual life an assured future may be. In a word, he did not yet understand the psychology of the horse who refuses to drink when taken to the water; and, noticing that public school men were, as a class, unintellectual, he assumed that their minds had been starved, and that their teachers set no store by intellect.

The idea of standing for a headmastership had first been suggested to him by an acquaintance whom chance had thrown in his way. After securing his Fellowship, Mr. Flaggon had accepted a post as tutor to a foreign prince, partly because the work was light and he needed a holiday, and partly because the tutorship was a travelling one and he was eager to see something of the world. Ten days of continuous rain and snow on the Riffel Alp had thrown him much into the society of the great man behind the scenes to whom allusion has already been made. The great man was both an enthusiast for education and a firm believer in ability; he even had the hardihood to maintain that ability is of greater value than experience, and experiment more fruitful of results than the accepted method of playing for safety. Being a shrewd judge of men, he soon discerned, beneath the tutor's quiet and unsensational exterior, signs of exceptional power; and he did not lose sight of him. The Welsh appointment was largely his doing, and, when the headmastership of Chiltern fell vacant, it was he who wrote and suggested that Mr. Flaggon should stand.

Mr. Flaggon himself had hardly regarded his candidature even as a forlorn hope. It was intended rather as a *ballon d'essai*, a notice to the scholastic world that he considered himself a possible headmaster, and an opportunity of gauging how that world would regard his claims. Chiltern, as we have seen, had no hesitation in branding his pretensions as presumptuous; and Mr. Flaggon was quite aware that the success of his audacious move, which had come as a surprise to himself, had been more a disappointment to his future colleagues.

But he was not dismayed by the difficulty of the task that lay before him. His whole life had been spent in overcoming difficulties, and he had the quiet confidence of a man who is sure of his own temper and accustomed to succeed. As has been stated before, he brought with him to his new work a great zeal for the cause of education; but he had no cut-and-dried theories of reform, no patent nostrum of his own. He knew what education *ought* to be, what it had been to himself – an individual renaissance, a quickening of the highest faculties of mind and spirit; and he knew that that was precisely what public school education was *not*. He was determined to study the problem on the spot and to proceed tentatively. The machinery, as he saw it, was antiquated, the bill of fare obsolete, the valley full of dry bones. But the dry bones were only waiting for a revivifying spirit to become clothed with flesh and to start into life again. In his mind's eye he saw the boys as hungry sheep who looked up and were not fed. He had not yet become acquainted with that particular breed of sheep that is born without an appetite.

But ever since his first flying visit to the school, Mr. Flaggon had begun to realise that there were other problems, behind the educational one, which would claim the attention of a headmaster. He had always taken on trust the virtues that are considered inherent in the public school system – loyalty, discipline, gentlemanly behaviour, and a subordination of the individual will to the interests of the community. In his undergraduate days he had often experienced an absurd sensation of being considered morally, as well as socially, inferior to the more fortunate alumni of the great public schools. Old Boys had talked to him with flashing eyes and genuine conviction of the exceptional merits of their own schools, and of the enhanced value which they gave to life; and he had believed them. And what he believed of other schools he had been taught to believe as pre-eminently true of Chiltern. Chiltern was the only institution of its kind about which nobody had as yet written a schoolboy story; but it ranked amongst the aristocracy of public schools, and, in the eyes of Chilternians, even higher. And it had special characteristics of its own. Somebody had said that Chiltern turned out gentlemen rather than scholars; and somebody else, probably an Old Chilternian, had added that you could always tell a Chiltern boy from the way he behaved in a drawing-room. Wealthy manufacturers sent their sons to Chiltern to acquire the easy manners and social polish which seemed natural to the place; and to be an Old Chilternian was an 'open sesame' to any club that was not primarily intellectual.

Mr. Flaggon had expected, therefore, to find a somewhat low level of mental attainments, but a high standard of good breeding. But ever since his first visit his mind had been haunted by the picture of three vapid youths strolling past their headmaster with insolent unconcern, and the blasé voices saying:

'Is that the new Gus?'

'Looks like it – unless it's his shuvver.'

And then there was the writing on certain walls in Mr. Cox's house.

This unfavourable impression was confirmed as he watched the boys in Chapel on the first Sunday of the Term. There was an air of insolence and swagger about the way in which the bigger boys strolled in last and lounged, instead of kneeling, during the prayers. Signs of intelligence were frequent between block and block; and, even among the smaller boys, there was often a kind of self-consciousness and pose, which, though he could not quite analyse the cause, affected Mr. Flaggon unpleasantly. He had often heard of the impressiveness of a school-chapel service. There was certainly nothing impressive about the service at Chiltern on the first Sunday of the Term, except, perhaps, the singing of the hymns – and that was much more noisy than reverent.

Mr. Flaggon belong to no definite party in the Church. A dislike of labels and definitions, coupled with a strong desire to make the Church inclusive rather than exclusive, had won him the easy hatred of the dogmatists and the reputation of being unorthodox. His own religious views had been deeply coloured by the life and example of his father, a man of great but unrecognised power, who had cheerfully sacrificed all personal ambition to work in an obscure Cumbrian parish. At one period of his youth, his father's attitude to life and cheerful acceptance of a lot so far below his merits, had puzzled him; and he had allowed himself to wonder whether such complete self-abnegation was commendable or even right. But the extraordinary manifestations of grief which that father's death provoked in the whole neighbourhood had taught him to judge the value of work by a different standard, and to realise that the things of the spirit can never be adequately measured in terms of the flesh. Henceforward, the life of duty, and faith in the individual conscience, which had been the secret of the father's influence, became the ideals of the son, and, if he was attracted into the field of education, it was largely because, to him, education in its truest sense meant a lifting of the veil from the spirit. But as he mounted the Chiltern pulpit to deliver his first sermon from the text 'The letter killeth, but the spirit maketh alive,' he felt conscious, instinctively and with something of a chill, that the note he was going to sound was not a note that would find an echo in the hearts of his congregation. Here were no hungry sheep looking up to be fed, but indifference, inertia, and an unknown something that was probably worse than either and possibly the cause of both.

Mr. Flaggon was an interesting and a distinguished preacher; his worst enemies admitted that. He had the gift of saying what he meant, the happy phrase, and the inevitable word. But if his manner could not but create a favourable impression, his matter caused serious alarm amongst the staff, and there was much shaking of heads afterwards in the great quadrangle under the shadow of Dr. Lanchester's statue.

'It's not so much the sermon,' said Mr. Pounderly in his most confidential tones; 'it's the text that frightens me. There were some points in the sermon, but the text was full of innuendo.'

'Surely,' exclaimed Mr. Bent, 'you are not going to hang a dog for his collar?'

'Pardon me!' said Mr. Pounderly, 'I hang no man. But unless my judgment is strangely at fault, that text, considering the time and the place, spells upheaval.'

'And the manner!' chimed in Mr. Beadle, 'the assured, precocious manner! The air of confidence and authority! I agree with Pounderly that we are marked down for slaughter; it is the death-knell of the Classics!'

And the two men walked off together shaking their heads.

Mr. Chowdler did not content himself with shaking his head afterwards in the great quadrangle. He shook it frequently and emphatically during the sermon, in order that everybody might know that he was in complete disagreement with the preacher. And on him fell the unpleasant duty, as he phrased it, of making a reply and restating the Lanchester position, on the third Sunday of the Term.

For, needless to say, Mr. Chowdler was in orders. No mere layman could have combined such a capacity for quarrelling with so profound a conviction of his own reasonableness and humility. In Mr. Chowdler's hands religion became a weapon to smite with. For choice, he smote lies, cant, humbug, and Bible critics; but occasionally quite innocent and respectable things found themselves floored by Mr. Chowdler's massive fist and trampled under his double-welted heel. For when Mr. Chowdler mounted the pulpit, necessity was laid upon him to smite something or somebody. There were men, like Mr. Plummer, who doubted whether there would be much scope in Heaven for Mr. Chowdler's type of religion; but, if they did not regard it as the highest form of Christianity, they had to admit that it was manly, and therefore good for the boys.

But on this third Sunday of the Term, Mr. Chowdler was no ordinary smiter; he was the incarnation of the Lanchester spirit repelling a German invasion. And his text, 'Hold fast to that which is good,' was not delivered like an ordinary text; it was fired like a six-inch shell full at the stall in which the headmaster was sitting. Mr. Bent said afterwards, that he fully expected to see Chowdler follow up the discharge of the text by leaving the cover of the pulpit and attacking with the bayonet. However, the preacher spoke daggers, but used none. Change? Yes, change was necessary, growth was necessary; but not change in essentials and axioms, not change in the foundations. Hold fast to the foundations, hold fast to that which is good! There was a tendency in a restless, riotous age to imagine that, because a thing lasted, because it was old and venerable, it was therefore obsolete. A fool's mistake! Why, granite lasts, gold lasts. Hold fast to the granite, hold fast to the gold, hold fast to that which is good. Again, there was a tendency in an age of feverish and futile activity to assail whatever is venerable, whatever has withstood the destructiveness of man and the storms of time. You tear up the mighty oak, and replace it by what? Tares? Yes, too often by tares, or at best by some finicking exotic treelet, such as you may see in gaudy Eastern pots in decadent drawing-rooms. Once more, hold fast to the mighty oak, hold fast to that which is good! Fortunately, and God be praised for it, they had in that place a great example by which to guide their endeavours – Abraham Lanchester, their great headmaster, restorer not destroyer, whose clear, sane intellect and genius, conservative in the best and noblest meaning of the word, had left them an imperishable birthright and a priceless heritage. Hold fast to a priceless heritage, hold fast to a great tradition, hold fast to that which is good! And so on for five-and-twenty minutes.

Mr. Flaggon was conscious that he was being preached at, and he knew that the boys knew it; for they kept turning round continually to see how he was taking it. Mrs. Chowdler, who watched him narrowly, maintained that he had been profoundly impressed and 'looked as if a new light had suddenly dawned on him'; but the general opinion among the boys was that he hadn't 'turned a hair' and that it was impossible to be sure whether he had really understood what 'Old Jowler' was driving at.

It is reasonable to suppose that the sermon gave Mr. Flaggon food for reflection; he certainly sat for some time afterwards in his study, looking into the fire and apparently thinking. But whatever his thoughts may have been, he kept them to himself and said nothing.

Mr. Chowdler's effort was much appreciated on the staff, even by some who were more prone to criticise than to praise. Mr. Pounderly pronounced it statesmanlike, and Mr. Black went so far as to say that it was inspired. Mr. Bent's was the only voice that called it 'bosh,' and he received a grave and well-deserved rebuke from Mr. Plummer for his lack of reverence. It was confidently assumed by many that Mr. Chowdler's serious note of warning, voicing, as it did, the general feeling of the staff, would give Mr. Flaggon pause and force him to recognise facts. But their optimism was of short duration; for within a few days, a notice asking every master to send in a copy of his weekly routine, made it clear to the most sanguine that the era of change and experiment had begun.

Chapter 5

MR. TIPHAM

It must be admitted that Mr. Flaggon was not uniformly lucky in his early experiments. This was notably the case in his first appointment to the staff. It has been already stated that he knew nothing of public schools from the inside, and in selecting a successor to Mr. Cox, he may have been too exclusively influenced by the claims of intellect and have taken too little account of other necessary qualifications. Anyhow, he thought that the intellectual side of the staff needed reinforcing, and, having a choice between a double first and double blue, he appointed the double first.

Mr. Tipham brought with him from Cleopas College, Cambridge, two more or less fixed ideas; first, that art consists in depicting disagreeable things in a disagreeable way, and secondly, that life in the twentieth century is governed by two conflicting forces – convention, which is always wrong, and Nature, which is always right. This theory had carried him not only safely but brilliantly through his university career. He had secured a first in both parts of the Tripos; he had played a prominent part in the life of his own college and been quoted outside it; he had worn strange clothes, founded a literary society in which thought was made to perform queer antics in shackles of its own imposing, and he had invented a new savoury. His slightly tilted nose and full cheeks gave him an air of confidence which unfriendly critics described as conceit, while the long brown hair, drawn back over the temples and plastered down with fragrant oils, the orange tie and loose green jacket, proclaimed that he was one of those for whom art is not merely a hobby but an integral part of life. One glance at his face would have informed any ordinarily shrewd observer that, in approaching new problems and unfamiliar ground Mr. Tipham would not suffer from diffidence. The late Victorians might have called him untidy and even unwashed; but at no period in English history would he have been branded as modest.

It was inevitable that Mr. Tipham should fall foul of the Lanchester tradition. He would have fallen foul of any tradition. But he chose to defy it in most unnecessary and offensive ways. He smoked as he walked down to school from his lodgings, he refused even a perfunctory homage to the claims of age and seniority, and the scarf that he wore almost permanently round his throat (for Mr. Tipham was an indoor man and sensitive to cold and damp) was a combination of colours – the colours of the Brainstorm Club – that shocked the moral sense of Chiltern by its unblushing æstheticism. Mr. Chowdler took a violent dislike to him at their first meeting, and missed no opportunity of trying to put him down by heavy sarcasm. But Mr. Tipham was an unsatisfactory butt; and when attacked he had a way of raising his eyebrows and inquiring 'How so?'

in a bored and superior tone, which goaded Mr. Chowdler to frenzy.

It was, indeed, soon evident that if the serious purpose of Mr. Tipham's life was to teach the boys, his recreation consisted in shocking the masters. To all the things that they held sacred, the very things that ought to have impressed him most, he applied the same disparaging term, 'mid-Victorian' or 'bourgeois'. Even the weekly dinner in Common Room, with its quaint ceremonial and unique endowment, did not escape the damning epithet. Before a fortnight had elapsed, everybody went about saying that that fellow Tipham was impossible.

Mr. Plummer, whose ideal (never, alas! to be realised in this world) was a united staff, and who was also the last man to abandon any sinner as irreclaimable, made a final and unsuccessful effort to bring about a better understanding. He gave a bachelor dinner-party, to which he invited a few of his own friends and the erring Mr. Tipham: for Mr. Plummer had a touching belief that if you can only bring mutually antagonistic people together over a glass of wine, they will learn to know and like each other.

Mr. Plummer occupied comfortable rooms in an old Georgian house that fronted the High Street. Bit by bit, and with a rare tact that spared natural susceptibilities, he had weeded out the furniture and pictures of his landlady and replaced them with his own. His taste was eclectic and eminently characteristic of pedagogic culture, and the inevitable photographs of the Hermes of Olympia and the Acropolis found a place of honour amongst the equally inevitable Arundels. His rooms were considered the best rooms in Chiltern, and he was not infrequently consulted by his colleagues on questions of art.

Mr. Tipham, for whose benefit Messrs. Bent, Rankin, Grady, and Chase had been brought together in the Georgian house, began the evening badly by arriving ten minutes late and in clothes which protested with unnecessary vehemence against the narrowness of convention. At Chiltern it was the custom, even at bachelor parties, for the guests to wear dress clothes; but Mr. Tipham scorned custom. A flannel shirt of that neutral tint which suggests either dirt or extreme age, a Norfolk jacket which might well have belonged to a tramp, and a pair of grey flannel trousers which the same tramp might conceivably have rejected, completed his festive attire, the only note of colour being provided by the bright orange tie which flamed beneath an unshaven chin. As Mr. Rankin said afterwards, he suggested a man who has snatched up some clothes hurriedly to run to the bathroom, rather than a guest at a dinner-party.

But Mr. Tipham was quite unconscious of the sudden drop in the temperature which followed his entry. He shot a rapid and critical glance round the room, and walking straight up to a small pastel drawing of a youth's head that hung on one of the walls, he tapped the glass lightly with his forefinger and inquired:

'Where did you get that?'

'That?' replied Mr. Plummer; 'oh, I picked that up at Chartres for a few francs; but I don't know that I care very much for it.'

'It's the best thing in the room,' said Mr. Tipham quietly; 'looks as if it might possibly be an early Creusot.'

Nobody but Mr. Tipham had ever heard of Creusot; so the remark was not taken up, and the party moved into the dining-room in depressed silence. At dinner it soon became apparent that Mr. Tipham was out to give instruction on other matters than art. The conversation had drifted, as conversation often did at Chiltern, on to the subject of boys. Mr. Grady had complained of their carelessness in handling chemicals, which resulted in frequent explosions, and their incapacity for anything like patient or systematic research; and Mr. Chase had pointed out the superiority of the Classics in this respect, in that they compelled a boy to think and left no room for experiment. 'You're both right and both wrong,' said Mr. Tipham with easy assurance. 'Chemistry can be made very interesting and the Classics very dull and *vice versa*. The truth is that, if you want to keep boys interested, you must make things lively. *I* always chip in for part of the time with something quite off the lesson. To-day I gave them a little lecture on Green Chartreuse.'

Mr. Plummer, who had long been struggling with a desire to snub tempered by a sense of his duties as a host, now cleared his throat and said, not without an effort:

'I suppose you had a good deal of experience before you came here?'

'No,' replied Mr. Tipham tartly; 'but I happen to have been a boy myself.'

And again the temperature fell by several degrees.

Mr. Bent had so far held himself in reserve, profoundly annoyed, yet watching with a certain cynical enjoyment the growing irritation of his colleagues and their inability to clothe it in appropriate words. But when, shortly afterwards, Mr. Tipham laid it down as an axiom that 'Dorian Gray' was the greatest work of art that the human intellect has ever produced, he saw his opportunity and began in his best ironic vein.

'It's refreshing to hear you say that; so few people ever venture, nowadays, to express old-fashioned opinions; and the Victorians seldom get justice done to them by the rising generation. I don't know that I agree with you on this particular point, but I am delighted to claim you as a Victorian.'

If there was one thing which Mr. Tipham disliked more than another it was to be indentified in any way with the Victorians; so he raised his eyebrows and said coldly, 'How so?'

If Mr. Bent had been wise he would have left well alone; as it was, he went on to embroider the theme a little recklessly. 'If one wants to be in the swim nowadays,' he said, 'one has to go into ecstasies over de Barsac or Roger Filkison. You read Roger Filkison, of course?'

Mr. Tipham admitted, with some reluctance, that he did not.

'Oh, he's the man, you know,' continued Mr. Bent, 'who writes the testimonials for the liver and kidney pills – the neo-realism they call it; very clever and morbid. I don't like it myself, but I know several Cambridge men who think it the most poignant literature since Verlaine.'

As Mr. Rankin and Mr. Grady were both Cambridge men, the pleasantry fell flat, and there was an awkward silence, till Mr. Tipham, lifting his eyebrows again, said in his most condescending manner:

'Ought one to be amused?'

And though Mr. Bent tried to look unconcerned, everybody realised that he had been rapped rather smartly over the knuckles. After this unfortunate incident there was a general feeling of constraint, which lasted through the rest of dinner. But when Mr. Chase has withdrawn to read prayers to his house, and cigars had been lit in the sitting-room, Mr. Tipham unbent once more and became enthusiastic over the merits of the post-impressionists – the dazzling designs of Van Googlen, the superb greens of Le Beaupère, and the masterly way in which Grummer painted flesh with one stroke of a glue-brush.

'I don't count him amongst the greatest masters,' said Mr. Bent, who had recovered his equanimity, 'because he can't paint pimples.'

'Perhaps,' replied Mr. Tipham loftily, 'you have never seen his "Lepers bathing."'

'No, I haven't,' said Mr. Bent warmly; 'and I can't say that I want to.'

'But in that case,' remarked Mr. Tipham, 'you are hardly in a position to judge, are you?'

Soon after ten, Mr. Bent, Mr. Rankin and Mr. Grady rose to go. Their host escorted them to the door with rather a wan look, for Mr. Tipham, instead of following their example, had just lit a fresh cigarette and dropped into the easy-chair vacated by Mr. Bent.

'Conceited idiot!' said Mr. Bent, when the three men were in the street.

'He has a lot to learn about boys,' added Mr. Grady, with a shake of his head.

'Wants a good scrubbing with soap and water, inside and out,' growled Mr. Rankin. 'But,' he added, afterwards, privately to Mr. Grady, 'old Bent didn't get much change out of him.'

As for Mr. Tipham, he continued to smoke cigarettes and instruct his host in the first principles of art till well after midnight.

Among the boys Mr. Tipham was generally regarded as a freak, and his nickname, 'The Super-tramp,' could hardly be regarded as flattering. But he had his disciples. Mind at Chiltern was held in little esteem, and, where it existed, uncongenial surroundings were apt to turn it sour. There were generally a few boys in the highest forms (for the most part boys of inferior physique and precocious interests) who were always in a state of latent revolt against a system which left them out of account. They repaid contempt with scorn, and the scorn was all the bitterer because it seldom dared to express itself in words and had to ferment inwardly.

To such boys Mr. Tipham appealed as a breath from a wider world and a champion of intellectual liberty. At the little dinners in his lodgings, at which a wine, which had the alluring title of a *petit vin blanc*, was followed by liqueurs, tongues were unloosed, and thought, if it was not always particularly clear, was at least delightfully audacious; and the crudest speculation passed for philosophy. Acting on a suggestion from their master, three of the disciples determined to found a school magazine in which Truth should at last find a voice. It must be admitted that the first and only number of 'Veritas' which saw the light, though not deficient in schoolboy humour, was unnecessarily personal and occasionally lacking in good taste. It contained obvious allusions to the headmaster, Mr. Grady, and many other members of the staff; but the most regrettable item of all was an imaginary interview, in which, under the transparent pseudonym of 'Howler,' Mr. Chowdler was held up to ridicule and contempt.

'Veritas' achieved a sensational but all too brief success. It sold like hot potatoes; but, within six hours of its publication, Mr. Chowdler appeared in the headmaster's study with thunder on his brow and a copy of the offensive journal in his hand. The venture had been anonymous; but the secret, like most school secrets, had been badly kept, and both the names of the editors and the complicity of Mr. Tipham were matters of common knowledge. Mr. Chowdler demanded that the editors should be made to apologise publicly before the whole school. As for what happened to Mr. Tipham, he did not care, for Mr. Tipham was beneath contempt; but the obvious course was probably the right one. In pressing his demand Mr. Chowdler was careful to explain that he was actuated by no desire for personal revenge; he was thinking only of discipline. At all costs discipline and the decencies of life must be preserved.

Mr. Flaggon was much annoyed by the whole occurrence. He had himself suggested to Mr. Tipham when appointing him, the idea of stimulating the boys to literary activity; but, needless to say, he had not intended the literary activity to take the form of a lampoon on Mr. Chowdler. However, he deprecated extreme measures and endeavoured to soothe the victim's ruffled feelings. The unsold copies of 'Veritas' were confiscated, and its further publication suppressed. Mr. Tipham, to borrow an expressive French phrase, 'had his head washed,' and the editors offered a full but private apology to Mr. Chowdler. But Mr. Chowdler was not satisfied. He maintained that 'the empty one' had behaved weakly to the boys and disloyally to himself. 'A paltry revenge,' he said, 'for my sermon.' Opinion on the staff was divided. Mr. Chase and the moderates thought that, on the whole, justice had been done. Mr. Pounderly and the irreconcilables considered that 'poor Chowdler' had been sacrificed. Nearly everybody was agreed that the headmaster was largely to blame; for he and he alone was responsible for appointing a man like Tipham – 'the Flaggonette,' as he was facetiously called. Mrs. Chowdler was quite bewildered.

'I cannot understand,' she said, 'how anyone can be so wicked and spiteful as to write such things about Harry, for everybody knows that my husband has gone out of his way to be kind and helpful to Mr. Tipham, as indeed he always does to all the new masters. And surely the headmaster must see that, by not supporting Harry and properly punishing the offenders, he will weaken his own position and make himself very unpopular; for the boys worship Harry.'

Chapter 6

THE CLOVEN HOOF

As Mr. Flaggon passed, one October afternoon, through the green door at the end of his garden, which led into Colonus, the air was full of voices that rose alternately to a frenzied shriek or dropped to a kind of monotonous chant. For the first round of house-matches was in progress and reputations were being lost and won.

Chiltern prided itself on being different from other schools, and Chiltern had a game of football peculiar to itself. It was a more manly game than any other code, and developed higher moral qualities in those who played it. As Mr. Chowdler said, no shirker, no humbug, could hope to win laurels at the Chiltern game.

When Mr. Chowdler's house was competing for laurels, Mr. Chowdler himself walked excitedly up and down the touch-line with a flushed face and protruding eyes, shouting, in a voice that dominated all others, instructions to his boys, such as 'Pass, Percy, pass! Feet, feet, Gerald! Shoot, Basil, shoot, can't you! Stick to it! Good lads all! Well *played*, Harry! Well played, sir!' For Mr. Chowdler always spoke to, and of, his boys by their Christian names. As a sort of tribal god, inspiring his children to deeds of valour, Mr. Chowdler was invaluable; but as a coach he had his limitations. For he had been brought up on the Rugby game and was never accepted as an authority on Chiltern football. Consequently his instructions were invariably ignored by the players. But he continued to shout them in perfect good faith, and they were regarded as an inevitable, if irrelevant, feature of the game.

Mr. Chowdler was in a good temper, for his house was winning easily, and Mr. Chowdler liked to win easily. An enthusiast for all forms of manly sport, he belonged to that particular brand of good sportsmen who find it easier to be chivalrous to a vanquished foe than fair to a victorious one. Accordingly, on the comparatively rare occasions on which his house was beaten, Mr. Chowdler always suspected the referee of partiality and his opponents of rough play; and, being an outspoken man, he did not keep his suspicions to himself. His own boys, less sensitive perhaps on the point of honour than their house-master, sometimes regretted these outbursts, which did not add to the popularity of the house.

But on the present occasion all was going well and Mr. Chowdler's temper was unruffled. The Chaseites (late Coxites) were only serving as a 'sullen ground' to show off the 'bright metal' of their adversaries. So, when he caught sight of Mr. Flaggon approaching, he left his post of observation on the touchline and went to meet him.

He was, indeed, feeling unusually well-disposed towards the new headmaster, for there had been a momentary rapprochement between the two men. Two days before, Mr. Chowdler had detected a boy in his Form cribbing – an offence about which he felt very strongly – and, acting on his advice, Mr. Flaggon had flogged the culprit; thus reverting to an old tradition which in the last seven years of Dr. Gussy's reign had become obsolete. With a clear lead of two goals his 'lads' could safely be left to their own devices for a few minutes, and it would be good for the new man to see the Chiltern game playing in the true Chiltern spirit and interpreted by one who was able to explain its ethical value. For, after all, there *might* be possibilities in the 'empty one,' and, rightly handled, he seemed not incapable of being taught.

Mr. Chase apparently thought so too. He was watching the defeat of his house with gloomy stoicism from the opposite side of the ground – a chivalrous Chowdler was always a little overwhelming – and, catching sight of the two men in earnest conversation, he nudged Mr. Bent, who was standing beside him, and whispered:

'See that? Chowdler's taking him in hand; same as poor old Gussy. Shouldn't wonder if some of our friends haven't been frightened with false fire after all.'

'H'm,' replied Mr. Bent. 'Appearances are often deceptive. Wait and see. Flaggon's a dark horse, and there'll be surprises yet.'

And the first of the surprises came about a week later at a house-masters' meeting. The meeting had been convened, nominally, for the purpose of discussing the scale of tradesmen's charges, which Mr. Flaggon thought excessive; but, at the close of it, he said in the most matter-of-fact way:

'As we are here, I should like to say a few words on another subject. I intend, in the more or less near future, to introduce certain changes into our curriculum with a view to making our teaching more effective. I don't know exactly yet what form those changes will take; but I have two things in my mind. In the first place, I find that our standard of scholarship is surprisingly low. I notice that last year we did not get a single scholarship of any importance at either university.'

'We have always discouraged pot-hunting here,' interrupted Mr. Pounderly. 'We have aimed at knowledge – not prizes.'

'I know,' said Mr. Flaggon; 'but there is the level of knowledge that I find so low here; much lower, for example, that it is in several other schools at which I have examined. And, in the second place, I am convinced that the average boy here (I am not speaking of the scholar) is not getting quite the kind of education which is best suited to his requirements.'

Mr. Flaggon paused, and if a pin had fallen it would have been distinctly audible, so tense was the silence. The challenge had been thrown down, but everybody waited for a moment to feel the edge of his weapon before rushing into the fray.

'I intend to do nothing rashly,' continued Mr. Flaggon. 'I wish the whole subject to be discussed thoroughly before we decide on anything final, so that every point of view may find its expression. And for that reason I think it would be interesting, and perhaps helpful, if we could obtain the views of at least some of our parents on the subject.'

There was a gasp; and Mr. Beadle, the authority on Plautus, rapped out:

'The parents have already expressed their views by sending their sons to Chiltern.'

'Not exactly,' said the headmaster. 'It all depends on what alternatives they had.'

'Surely,' pleaded Mr. Pounderly, 'surely, to call in the parents would be like calling in the patient to advise the specialist.'

'I don't think so,' said Mr. Flaggon. 'The truer analogy would be to say that we are like the specialist who consults the patient's relatives about the patient's symptoms. And the relatives are often able to give very helpful information to the specialist.'

'Do I understand you to propose,' said Mr. Chowdler in a voice of concentrated irony, 'that we should call in their uncles and cousins and aunts and make a regular symposium of it?'

Mr. Flaggon winced, but he kept his temper.

'I don't think,' he said, 'that in this case there would be any practical advantage in going beyond the parents. What I wanted to say was, that I shall be very grateful if house-masters will let me have the names and addresses of any representative parents who are likely to be interested in such a proposal. I thought perhaps that we might arrange to meet them, quite informally, some time in November or at the beginning of December.'

'What exactly do you mean by a representative parent?' asked Mr. Flyte, with the air of a man who is putting a poser.

'I must really leave that to the discretion of house-masters,' replied Mr. Flaggon, with a smile.

News of the impending parents' committee ran through the staff like fire through gorse, and soon all Chiltern was ablaze. Some called it the thin edge of the wedge; others, the cloven hoof. The Liberals (for there were a few Liberals even at Chiltern) said that Flaggon was setting up a Second Chamber to override the decisions of Masters' Meetings; the Conservatives, that he was appealing to Demos. All agreed that the innovation was a blow to the prestige of the masters and an infringement of their ancient rights. Even Mr. Plummer felt and spoke strongly, and he imparted his fears to Mr. Bent, as they were taking the hill walk, commonly known as the 'Ushers' Grind,' one sunny autumn afternoon.

The friendship of Mr. Bent and Mr. Plummer was founded on a complete dissimilarity of tastes. It is true that they shared a dislike of golf and motors, but in all other respects they were in hearty disagreement. Mr. Plummer's faith in man goaded Mr. Bent almost into violence, and Mr. Bent's distrust of human nature in general, and middle-class human nature in particular, filled Mr. Plummer with righteous indignation. At the end of every walk the nerves of each were raw and tingling; but they never failed to walk together twice or even thrice in the course of every week. The particular form of quarrelling in which they indulged had grown upon them like a drug habit, and neither could do without it for long.

A stranger who knew them by reputation, but not by sight, would inevitably have mistaken each for the other. Mr. Plummer, tall and thin, with a hooked nose, hollow cheeks, and sallow complexion, looked the embodiment of pessimism; while Mr. Bent, short, stout, with round eyes and a florid face, ought to have been a born optimist. Mr. Rankin used to say that Providence had designed the character of the one for the person of the other, that a malicious fairy had negotiated an exchange, and that they sought each other's company because, apart, they were both conscious of being incomplete.

But on this occasion, as we have said, Mr. Plummer was inclined to be pessimistic.

'I don't like this idea,' he said, 'of calling in an outside opinion. If the parents once get it into their heads that they are able to dictate, there will be an end of systematic teaching.'

'My good Plummer,' replied Mr. Bent, 'there cannot possibly be an end, because there has never been a beginning. Systematic teaching indeed! Why, a boy told me the other day that he had been doing the same French book ever since he came to the school two years ago; and it is notorious that Cox set one and the same Latin prose every term to his Form, and never looked it over.'

'I was not thinking of organisation,' said Mr. Plummer, 'I was speaking of principles; and I repeat, if the parents are allowed to dictate the lines on which education is to proceed, there will be an end of systematic teaching.

'They will not dictate', said Mr. Bent; 'they have no manuscript to dictate from. Their theories on education are purely negative – I say, steady up the hill! The only thing they insist on is that their offspring should not be taught to think or know. Thought and knowledge are dangerous to the existing social order and must be smothered young, like the Princes in the Tower. Provided that they *are* smothered, the parents don't care a rap what sort of a pillow is used.'

'Thought,' said Mr. Plummer, 'hardly exists outside the middle-classes.'

'Knowledge,' retorted Mr. Bent, 'only begins where middle classdom ends. The art of being middle class consists in shutting yourself up in a detached house and only recognising the people who come in at the front door. Knowledge leads to the back door and the streets, and is therefore fatal to the art; and knowledge is the goal of education.'

'If parents didn't believe in education,' said Mr. Plummer, 'they would't send their boys here.'

'The English middle classes,' said Mr. Bent, 'never have believed in education. The Scotch did once, till they discovered the superior merits of football; but the English never. And they send their sons here to be inoculated against it – I say, *do* go a bit slower. For choice they put them with Chowdler, who returns them, in a few years, finished specimens of Philistinism, with orthodox views on Bible criticism and the off-theory, and a complete lack of interest in anything that really matters.'

'I don't at all agree with you,' said Mr. Plummer; 'but if the parents are such hopeless idiots as you describe them, why do you want to consult them?'

'I don't,' replied Mr. Bent. 'But if they are such angels of light as you imagine them, why do you object to asking for their advice?'

'You are paradoxical,' snapped Mr. Plummer.

'And you are illogical,' panted Mr. Bent.

Chapter 7

THE AFFAIR OF LE WILLOW

WHILE Mr. Chowdler was lamenting that discipline was going to the dogs, the boys were beginning to complain that liberty was being destroyed. Some of them went so far as to maintain that Chiltern was becoming a regular preparatory school. For not only were motor-bicycles forbidden (they had always been *that*), but it was becoming positively dangerous to ride them. Moreover, detection entailed consequences. In the palmy days of Dr. Gussy it had been the ambition of every boy, caught in a misdemeanour, to be reported to the headmaster; and the appeal from summary justice to Cæsar had been one of the most cherished privileges of Chiltern whilst Dr. Gussy was Cæsar. For Dr. Gussy believed in talking – earnest, practical, confidential talking. As the boys said, 'Gus treated you like a gentleman'; whereas Flaggon – there was no pleasure, nothing morally bracing, about an interview with Flaggon.

And other offences besides motor-biking were being detected with alarming frequency. Masters, who had hitherto been regarded as quite inoffensive, seemed to take a pleasure in appearing where they were least expected. The truth is that, having less belief in Dr. Gussy's talks than Dr. Gussy himself, they had got into the habit of purposely avoiding knowledge which they knew would lead to no result; but, finding that Mr. Flaggon was prepared to act as well as talk, they resumed their normal activities.

No inconsiderable factor in the growing absence of security was the disappearance of 'Whisky Toddler', the college porter. When he paid his surprise visit to Chiltern in the holidays, Mr. Flaggon had been conscious of a subtle aroma about the place, which ceased suddenly when he took leave of the porter; and the suddenness of the change had set him wondering whether the extreme solemnity of Mr. Todd was due solely to wisdom or was partly induced by alcohol. The wonder did not diminish on closer acquaintance, and an unexpected visit to the Lodge, one evening, settled all doubts. Mr. Todd was found in a state of hilarious incoherence. It was, of course, an accident – a toothache, and an old-fashioned remedy, recommended by a friend, which had produced unforeseen results in one unused to spirituous liquors. Mr. Todd refused with quiet dignity to purchase the chance of reinstatement by taking the pledge and spending a month in a home for inebriates. He preferred to retire, at once, on a quarter's salary and a small pension.

The boys, of course, had always known that 'Whisky Toddler' drank like a fish; but opinion on the staff was acutely divided. There is no question that has so many sides to it as drink, nor one about which it is so hard to arrive at any convincing conclusion. The very fact that Mr. Todd's nose was red and his eyes watery was, to some, a proof of his innocence. For people are sure to say that a man with a red nose and watery eyes drinks; whereas anyone *may* have a red nose and weak eyes without drinking, and it is horribly unfair that a man should be treated as a moral leper because of some physical infirmity. There were many, therefore, besides Mr. Plummer, who believed, and still believe, that poor Todd was 'hardly treated'; and poor Todd said nothing to discourage their belief.

His place was taken by a man of unprepossessing manners and abrupt activity – Pigeon was his name. There was a certain mystery about his past. Some said that he had once been a spy in the pay of the Russian police; others, that he had been a proctor's bulldog at Oxford; others, that he had been a Scotland Yard detective. At all events, there could be no doubt that it was as a detective that he was brought by the 'New Gus' to Chiltern. A porter is assumed to possess tact; but Pigeon had none – no gift of shutting his eyes on occasions when eyes are better shut. And so it came to pass that he discovered Mr. Chowdler's Prætor smoking among the rhododendrons in Colonus, and reported him to the headmaster.

At Chiltern the captain of every house was called its 'Prætor' and
wielded vast authority. In a post for which character was the prime
consideration, position in the school was only of secondary importance.
Hence it happened that, though Le Willow had with difficulty fought his
way into the senior Fifth, he was Prætor of Mr. Chowdler's house. But,
though not distinguished intellectually, he was captain designate of the
eleven for the succeeding year, a very fair change bowler, and a bat with
a most taking style. He enjoyed the entire confidence of his house-master
and the respect of his fellows. It was regrettable, therefore, from every
point of view, that he should have been smoking behind the
rhododendrons in Colonus; and still more regrettable that, having been
smoking, he should have been discovered.

Enough has been said already of Mr. Chowdler to make it clear that
he was adamantine on the question of discipline. But it was a matter of
common observation amongst his colleagues that his attitude toward
offences underwent a considerable change when the offender was one
of his own boys. This is a species of infirmity to which parents and
house-masters are peculiarly liable. In Mr. Chowdler's case it took the
form of a conviction that, though 'his lads' might be technically in the
wrong, they were morally quite sound; and he always held that
punishment ought to take account of the character of the offender. He
was really pained by Le Willow's 'thoughtlessness'; but there were
extenuating circumstances. The boy was encouraged to smoke at home,
and he had one of those muddled old heads that find it so difficult to
draw the distinction between home and school; especially when the
home is a good one. The poor old fellow had admitted to him
(Chowdler), with a shake of his poor old head and a look in his poor old
eyes which was really pathetic, that he knew he was a 'blighted ass'. He
was, in fact, just the kind of boy for whom justice should be tempered
with mercy.

All this, and more, Mr. Chowdler said to the headmaster on behalf of
his Prætor, and he was profoundly shocked when Mr. Flaggon, after
listening attentively to the counsel for the defence, announced that he was
going to deprive Le Willow of his Prætorship and Prefectship, not merely

temporarily, but for the term of his natural life. 'I fail to see where the mercy comes in,' growled Mr. Chowdler.

'Perhaps in my not flogging him into the bargain,' replied Mr. Flaggon. 'But, really, I don't consider this a case for mercy. The boy is in a position of trust. Five days ago I called the Prefects together and spoke to them about their duties, especially the duty of setting a good example: and I mentioned smoking by name. All the circumstances aggravate the offence. I have no right to be merciful.'

'But probably he didn't understand,' pleaded Mr. Chowdler. 'You don't know what a business it is to drive any idea into that poor, thick old head of his. The boy's as honest as the daylight, but terribly obtuse.'

'If he can't understand a plain speech and a plain duty,' replied Mr. Flaggon, 'he is certainly not fit to exercise power.'

'You can't prevent a boy with such athletic gifts and such a sunny nature from exercising power by any official ukase,' said Mr. Chowdler, with increasing warmth. 'If you destroy his self-respect by a punishment which he feels to be unjust, you take away from him all motives for doing right; you drive him into evil courses.'

'I intend my Prefects to govern,' replied Mr. Flaggon; 'and you can never get men or boys to act responsibly unless you visit grave breaches of duty on them heavily. I am sorry for Le Willow, if he is all that you describe him; but I cannot alter my decision.'

'You admit then,' snapped out Mr. Chowdler, 'that you are sacrificing the boy to an abstract theory.'

'I admit nothing of the kind,' said Mr. Flaggon.

A good many of the masters, who did not share Mr. Chowdler's enthusiasm for Le Willow, approved of the headmaster's action; and, though they did not say so publicly, were not sorry to see Mr. Chowdler's straying sheep treated for once in a way like other people's straying sheep. But Mr. Chowdler himself made no attempt to conceal his displeasure either from masters or boys.

'I don't call that kind of thing discipline,' he said; 'I call it panic. A strong man doesn't hit about wildly without caring where the blow falls. With all his faults, dear old Gussy was never unjust. Le Willow's too good an old fellow at bottom to be soured for long or lose his sunny nature. But that's how criminals are made.'

Mr. Chowdler's views received a striking corroboration, at least in his own eyes, when three weeks later, Le Willow was caught cribbing. It is true that Mr. Bent, his Form master, had suspected him for the greater part of two terms; but, as Mr. Plummer said, suspicion proves nothing. In the midst of his grief Mr. Chowdler was almost triumphant.

'What did I tell you,' he exclaimed. 'You can see now for yourselves. That's how boys are driven into evil courses.'

But the headmaster, instead of recognising the folly of his ways and apologising to Mr. Chowdler and his ex-prætor, decided that, after his second offence, the boy could not remain in the school and must leave at the end of the term.

Dismiss the captain of next year's eleven, a bat with the most taking style that had been seen at Chiltern since the days of Goring who played for England, and a very fair change bowler into the bargain! All Chiltern was aghast, and even Mr. Chase, who usually had something to say on behalf of the headmaster, admitted that it was an act of doubtful wisdom.

To Mr. Chowdler it was not merely an act of doubtful wisdom, it was a travesty of justice, an outrage, a scandal – in fact almost any strong word that you can think of. When a man thinks as strongly as Mr. Chowdler thought about some gross miscarriage of justice, it is impossible for him to keep his feelings to himself; he would rather be guilty of indiscretion than of a criminal silence; and soon boys, masters, and the parents and relatives of the victim, were in full possession of Mr. Chowdler's opinions on the subject.

Le Willow was well connected; in fact, as Mrs. Chowdler put it, he had a grandfather; and the grandfather wrote a letter to the chairman of the Council which caused that gentleman much concern. He wanted to know why the dickens they had appointed to Chiltern a headmaster who didn't know the ABC of his profession. Expel from school a promising lad for a boyish offence of which they had all been guilty, probably, in their day! The thing was absurd. Boys and masters alike were in a state of mutiny; and he called upon the chairman to intervene.

The chairman was perplexed; for the grandfather was no ordinary grandfather but a man with a commanding name and a great social position. After some hesitation he wrote to the headmaster, disclaiming any idea of interfering, but asking for information. He wished, he said, to be in a position to contradict certain reports, unfounded no doubt, which were being circulated in the London clubs and which might damage the school.

Thus appealed to, Mr. Flaggon wrote a detailed account of the affair and of the principles which had guided his own action. He added that the tone and discipline of Chiltern were very different from what he had been led to expect, and that Le Willow, besides being somewhat old for his place in the school, was not a desirable asset.

The chairman shook his head dubiously over this communication and murmured something about 'new brooms' and 'excess of zeal'; but he informed the grandfather with much tact that, though the Council felt great sympathy with him, they were unable to interfere in a matter that directly concerned the discipline of the school, and that any appeal for mercy must be made to the headmaster in person. As for Le Willow, he was sure that the boy had a brilliant future in front of him, and he wished him every success.

And there the matter ended, except that the Le Willow parents cursed Mr. Flaggon by all the Le Willow gods and threatened to bring an action; which threat they were wise enough not to carry into effect. Also that Lord Chalvey withdrew his son who was entered for Mr. Chowdler's house in the following term. This was a contingency which Mr. Chowdler had not foreseen when he started on his campaign, and it did not help to reconcile him to the headmaster.

And, while the chairman was actually penning his reply to the duke, one wet November afternoon, Mr. Plummer and Mr. Bent were once more pacing the 'Ushers' Grind' in mackintoshes. A steady drizzle had damped their fighting spirit, and taunts that usually kindled flames had only produced a perfunctory fizzle. At last Mr. Plummer said:

'I'm afraid the boys haven't a great respect for Flaggon.'

'I shouldn't take Chowdler too seriously,' said Mr. Bent.

'I didn't say Chowdler,' replied his companion; 'I said the boys.'

'I know you did,' said Mr. Bent. 'And *I* said Chowdler, because I bet that he has been telling you his story of the week – we have all heard it – to wit, how little Simpkin looked up at him with a wistful smile and said, "Sir, do you think the new headmaster understands anything about boys?"'

'Suppose he did!' said Mr. Plummer defiantly. 'What then?'

'Only,' replied Mr. Bent, 'that it isn't a *very* likely thing for a boy to say, on his own. I know little Simpkin; he's in my Form. All Chowdler's pets are in my Form. A nasty, greasy, oily little beast. He tried "the wistful" on with me once, but never again.'

'The fact that you think him oily and greasy,' retorted Mr. Plummer, 'is no proof that he didn't say it.'

'I never said it was,' cried Mr. Bent, raising his voice, 'and I don't doubt that little Simpkin *did* say it and will say it again till he gets another cue. What *does* amaze me is that, with all his experience, Chowdler has never learned that boys encourage us in our illusions by quoting at us our own pet ideas and phrases. It isn't conscious hypocrisy – merely an instinct of self-preservation, or an amiable desire to please. They approach us, as *we* should approach some beast of uncertain temper, with the sounds that experience has shown to be most soothing.'

'So you have said before,' snorted Mr. Plummer. 'But, anyhow, you admit that Chowdler has experience; and Flaggon has none.'

'Pooh! Experience indeed!' cried Mr. Bent contemptuously. 'What's experience? A snare and a delusion, unless you can bring an unbiassed mind to bear on it; which schoolmasters never can. The man who looks at this view, for the first time, with the naked eye, sees far more of it than the man who looks at it for the hundredth time through smoked glasses. Experience is the smoke on the glasses; it's the cure of our profession. We are all much more efficient when we're young than we ever are afterwards. Give *me* the young and inexperienced man.'

'Tipham, for example,' said Mr. Plummer drily.

'Oh, Tipham's an exception,' replied Mr. Bent airily. 'Tipham never *was* young. He was born with a greased head, grey flannel trousers, and a terror of being thought sane. But I can tell you, Chowdler was ten times more efficient as a master fifteen years ago, when you and I first came to the school, than he is now. We all become progressively greater idiots as we grow ripe in experience.'

'Bosh!' said Mr. Plummer.

Chapter 8

THE PARENTS' COMMITTEE

ON the last day of November the much-talked-of Parents' Committee met. Mr. Flaggon's attention had been so fully occupied by other and more pressing affairs that he had not had time to prepare for the event as carefully as he could have wished. Indeed, the purely educational problem had lately taken a less prominent place in his mind. But some dozen parents had shown themselves sufficiently interested in the proposal to promise their personal support; and of these, seven actually put in an appearance on the appointed day. They included Lady Bellingham, a recognised authority on Women's Education, and Sir Philip Whaley, senior partner in a great commercial house, director of several flourishing companies, and a person of considerable importance in the city. A successful stockbroker, who happened to be visiting his boy at Chiltern on the day, was pressed, reluctantly, into the service at the eleventh hour and made the numbers even. The meeting was held in the library, a handsome room that opened out of the Great Hall, and was intended to be quite informal. The masters had all been invited to attend, but, as attendance as optional, a great many of them marked their disapproval by staying away. A sense of duty, however, brought Mr. Plummer and about a dozen others to this new kind of Parliament, and Mr. Bent was present, as he expressed it, for the sheer fun of the thing.

The headmaster stated in a few words the object of the gathering, and Lady Bellingham opened the debate. Lady Bellingham was the star of the occasion, and she had come provided with a typewritten paper which she proceeded to read with evident gusto. It was rather a lengthy paper, and before it was over Sir Philip Whaley and the stockbroker were seen to yawn surreptitiously. The gist of it was that children should be brought up among beautiful things in order that what is beautiful in them may be fostered and developed. Nature is always beautiful, and in educating the young we must trust more to Nature and less to artificial restrictions. We must not interfere with a beneficent purpose, and Nature's purposes are always beneficent. 'Nursed on the great bosom of Nature' beautiful children will grow up into beautiful men and women.

When Lady Bellingham had finished, Mr. Bent, assuming his most impressive and deferential manner, asked if he might put a question.

'Certainly,' replied Lady Bellingham affably.

'I do not press,' said Mr. Bent, 'for any definition of what you call "beautiful things," because that might introduce the personal element. But when you urge that we should impose no restrictions on Nature, I foresee difficulties. Measles, for example, are a form of Nature, and of course you would not wish us to impose no restrictions on measles.'

'Of course not,' said Lady Bellingham, with amused pity.

'Then might I ask,' said Mr. Bent, 'what exactly we are to understand by Nature?'

'Nature,' replied Lady Bellingham, 'is impossible to define. It is too vast, too varied. But, roughly speaking, whatever is beautiful is natural, and whatever is ugly is unnatural.'

'I see,' said Mr. Bent.

Then Sir Philip Whaley, who had long been chafing under an enforced silence, took up his parable and spoke. Sir Philip possessed, in an unusual degree, the charm of English oratory – the gift, that is, of emphasising and repeating the obvious and connecting his rounded phrases with ornamental 'ums' and 'ers.'

'You must look at education,' he began, 'from what I venture to call the business point of view. You schoolmasters are too inclined, if you will forgive me for saying so, to ignore, to leave out of account, the – um – er – the business point of view. But, if you are going to think Imperially, if, that is, you are going to think in terms of Empire, in terms, I say, of Empire, you cannot leave the business point of view out of account – um – er – you must take it into your calculations. For behind the Imperial problem, lies the business problem. We city men are familiar with this truth, it is a matter of common knowledge amongst us; but it is one of the things that you schoolmasters, if you will pardon me for saying so, are inclined to leave out of account.'

'You are forgetting Nature,' interrupted Lady Bellingham.

'Pardon me, madam,' replied Sir Philip, 'I am *not* forgetting Nature, but I am looking at it from the practical point of view – from what I have ventured to call the business point of view. Let me give you a concrete instance of what I mean.' Here Sir Philip dropped his voice to a confidential tone. 'When I have a post in my office to fill – I am speaking, mind you, of a post with prospects attached to it, a real chance for a young fellow – um – er – well, what kind of a man do I want to fill it? A scholar? No. A man who can read Homer and write Latin verses? No. I am saying nothing against Homer as Homer, mark you, but I am considering the thing from the practical point of view. What *I* want is a man who has learned shorthand and can write commercial French – um – er – and I don't find him – that's the point – I don't find him in the public schools or the universities; as often as not I am obliged in the end to bring in a foreigner – a German. That's where the Germans are ahead of us. Well, there you have it in a nutshell. The public schools of England are not seriously training their boys to take their proper place in the business life of the Empire; and the Germans are. That,' he concluded, bringing his fist down on the table in front of him, 'that is what I mean by saying that you ought to look at education from the business point of view. I hope I have made myself clear.

Sir Philip wiped his brow and looked around with a complacent smile. The headmaster, whose face while the city oracle was speaking had been a study, made no comment; but Mr. Bent leaned forward with knitted brows and began:

'I have been much interested in what Sir Philip Whaley has been telling us, but I am not sure whether I interpret him correctly. Do I understand him to say that he wishes shorthand and commercial French to form a necessary part of the school curriculum?'

'I do,' said Sir Philip, 'most certainly I do.'

'I realise,' continued Mr. Bent, 'that for anybody who is aspiring to a post in Sir Philip Whaley's office, shorthand and commercial French are a necessary branch of culture. But what about the boys who are going in for the learned or other professions – the Church, for example? Might not commercial French be, to a future bishop, what Homer is to Sir Philip himself, an ornamental but irrelevant accomplishment? And we must not ignore the bishops.'

'You must specialise,' said Sir Philip grandly. 'You must be prepared to fit every boy with the special knowledge that he – um – er – will require in the profession of his choice. You schoolmasters, if you will forgive me for saying so, do not sufficiently realise the importance of specialising.'

'The difficulty of specialising beyond a certain point,' said Mr. Flaggon, 'lies in the additional expense: and public school education is costly enough already. Our problem is to find a common basis of education for all.'

Sir Philip was not accustomed to have his judgments disputed, and he met the objection by repeating his previous remarks with amplifications. When he had finished for the second time, a Mrs. Sparrow, who had been making chirruping little noises to herself all the while, seized the opportunity to say that, for want of somebody better, she had come to represent the mothers' point of view; and what mothers cared most about were just the little things that men so often didn't notice. She was sure that the food was all that could be wished for or desired, and she wasn't for a moment complaining about *that*. But she did think that the boys weren't given enough time to eat in. She was horrified at the way her own boy had learned to gobble his food in the holidays, and all doctors were agreed about the importance of eating slowly and biting properly. That was one thing. And, then, she did think that, for a big school, the sick-house was *rather* a dreary place – such bare unfurnished rooms and floors. When her boy was ill last Easter Term and she came down to see him, she went away feeling quite depressed.

Of course everybody was *most* kind, and she knew that the school doctor was a very clever man; but she did think that the sick-house might be made a little more cheerful. That was the mothers' point of view, and she hoped that Mr. Flaggon would not mind her putting it; for, after all, a mother *did* know more about her own children than anybody else did.

Mr. Flaggon said that he was always delighted to hear what the mothers had to say, and he would give due weight to Mrs. Sparrow's suggestions; but he thought that they were perhaps straying a little beyond the scope of the meeting, and he invited the other parents to give their views on the main subject under discussion, namely, education.

The other parents, thus appealed to, explained that they had come to listen and not to talk; but the stockbroker, who had from the first exhibited symptoms of acute boredom, remarked that, as he was there, he might as well say what he knew that most people thought, though apparently they were afraid to say so. 'If you ask me,' he said, leaning back in his chair and thrusting his thumbs into the armholes of his waistcoat, 'if you ask me, I don't think it matters a rap *what* you teach 'em. When I was at school, *I* never did a stroke of work – had a jolly good time, and I can't say that I'm sorry for it. And I'm worth now' (here Mr. Flaggon winced visibly) – 'well, it doesn't matter what I'm worth; but I know that I could buy up half the swots – that's what we used to call them in my days – half the swots who worked 'emselves silly over their Latin and Greek and all that sort of gibberish. And when I sent my youngster here, I said to him: "You may work if you like; you can please yourself about that, and it's a point you'll have to settle with your masters; but, if you want to please your dad, remember that I'd a da– jolly sight sooner see you head of your eleven than head of the school."That's what I said; and I don't believe, Mr. Headmaster, that you've got a finer little sportsman in your school than my youngster.'

Long before the discussion was over Mr. Flaggon realised that it had been a mistake and would only give the enemy cause to blaspheme. And he was not mistaken. Lady Bellingham was the joy of Common Room for weeks afterwards, and it was humorously assumed that she had made a convert of the headmaster. When a new chimney appeared on the Lodge, everybody said, 'Flaggon is surrounding us with beautiful things'; when the rhododendrons at the far end of Colonus were thinned out, it was 'Flaggon is uncovering the great bosom of Nature.' And again, when a notice came round about the wearing of great-coats, somebody remarked that Flaggon was looking at education from the mothers' point of view. Mr. Chowdler, who had not been present at the meeting, picked up all the best things and added them to his repertory. In fact, there was a regular carnival of wit, and the wags had the time of their lives.

Only Mr. Bent affected to be agreeably surprised. 'They were,' he said, 'an unusually intelligent set of parents – quite unusually intelligent. Lady Bellingham, of course, talked an amazing lot of drivel; you would expect that from a woman. Still, she knows a great deal more than Chowdler does; for though she can't express herself rationally, she does realise in a vague way that beauty is a form of truth, and that education ought to mean something more than Balbus-built-a-wall and the off-theory. Even Mr. – I can't remember his name – the stockbroker, has grasped what education is *not*; which is more than Chowdler ever has. They offered him an inferior substitute at the school where he spent his dazzling youth, and, with the intuition of genius, he divined that it was not worth his acceptance. And probably it wasn't. And, then, the silent ones! How seldom you find four people in any given room who are wise enough to keep silence about a subject of which they know nothing. Whaley was the only really hopeless failure. Yes, they certainly were an unusually intelligent set of parents.'

'That's all very well,' protested Mr. Plummer, 'but if *I* had said so, you would have cursed me for my unreasoning optimism and made out that I was blinded by my infatuation for the middle classes.'

'Perhaps,' replied Mr. Bent airily, 'perhaps. And very likely I should have been right.'

Chapter 9

'GOD'S IN HIS HEAVEN'

'I ALWAYS wonder, Bent,' said Mr. Rankin, as the two men met in Colonus on their way to the ground where the Cock-house match was about to begin – 'I always wonder why you, who pour such scorn on athleticism, never by any chance miss a house-match.'

'There are many things in this world to wonder at,' replied Mr. Bent; 'for instance, why the sea is boiling hot and why Radicals are the most inveterate Tories in private life. But, as a matter of fact, it is not the football that attracts me on these occasions so much as the psychology of the competing house-masters.'

'Translate with brief notes,' said his companion.

'To an observer of human nature,' Mr. Bent explained, 'nothing is so illuminating as the behaviour of a house-master when his house is playing a match. Chowdler, of course, is elemental, and offers few points of interest; he has the naked simplicity of the savage or the sportsman – blatant in victory, ungenerous in defeat. But Trimble is more complex, and, therefore, more worthy of study. If I join him, he will affect an air of complete detachment and ask me for my views on Welsh Disestablishment or Woman Suffrage; but he will interrupt himself at intervals to murmur "Fools! asses! idiots! they deserve to be beaten!" Of course they *will* be beaten?'

'Don't be too sure of that!' said Mr. Rankin. 'Two of Chowdler's best men are crocked, and Trimble's have come on a lot lately.'

'Chowdler being beaten,' said Mr. Bent, 'is a much more amusing spectacle than Chowdler winning. But I don't regard it as possible. He always keeps a reserve force – a kind of territorial army – of lean and hungry veterans with Christian names, who have grown old in the service of their country. I am credibly informed that his senior fag, whom I see on the field, is a widower and maintains a family of four at Brighton. They all belong to the class which Chowdler designates as "poor old" or "good old"; and against this combination of age, godliness, and thrift, no ordinary house eleven stands a chance.'

'Don't talk rot,' said Mr. Rankin. '*I* back Trimble's. They'll take a lot of beating to-day.'

The whole school and most of the masters were out to watch the game. Mr. Tipham was conspicuous in his post-impressionist scarf, shouting ostentatiously for Trimble's. Mr. Grady hovered uneasily on the outskirts, with the hunted look on his face; perhaps the noise reminded him of his more uproarious classes. Mrs. Chowdler and Mrs. Trimble were seated in a reserved enclosure, exchanging feline amenities. Their better halves wandered about on opposite sides of the ground – Mr. Chowdler on the touch-line, Mr. Trimble a little in the rear of the spectators, in a state of internal agitation which would have made sitting impossible. For the game was of a most thrilling description. In the first half Trimble's did most of the attacking and crossed over with a lead of one goal to nothing.

'Oh, it's all right!' said Mr. Trimble with assumed nonchalance to Mr. Bent, who had just congratulated him on the results so far obtained. 'We shall go to pieces sure enough in the second half; my fellows have a perfect genius for collapsing. The asses! If they hadn't bungled all their chances we might have been three up.'

It looked as if Mr. Trimble's gloomy prophecy was going to be fulfilled; for the game had hardly been restarted when a foolish misunderstanding among the Trimbleite backs enabled Chowdler's to equalise; and, before their opponents had recovered from the shock and consequent demoralisation, Le Willow sent in a lucky shot which put his side ahead. A yell of triumph went up from the Chowdlerites and their supporters, and Mr. Chowdler himself, in spite of a heavy fur coat, leapt into the air on the touch-line and beat his gloved hands one against the other.

'Well played, Harry!' he roared. 'Well played all! Good lads! Stick *to* it, stick *to* it!'

'Given away with a pound of tea!' said Mr. Trimble with a short mirthless laugh. 'That settles the game; and I must say that we thoroughly deserve to lose. Did you ever see such football!'

Mr Trimble, though he was one of the best house-masters at Chiltern, was a man of rather insignificant appearance. The youngest Miss Gussy had once said of him that he always looked as if he were wearing somebody's else's cast-off clothes. On this particular afternoon he had on an ulster of antique design and faded yellow colour, which contrasted unfavourably with the smart fur coat of his rival and seemed to brand him as of inferior rank.

'The moral effect of that last goal,' said Mr. Bent, whose sympathies were with the ulster, 'may be disastrous; but the game is not over yet. I must confess that I am beginning to be horribly excited. I have not got your philosophic detachment, Trimble; and the sight of Chowdler on the touch-line, clapping his great woollen gloves together, always arouses most unchristian feelings in me. I want to see him, not merely beaten, but crushed, disgraced, annihilated. Well played! Oh, well played!'

For the Trimbleites, stung by disaster, had roused themselves to superhuman efforts and were once more attacking fiercely. There was a confused *mêlée* in front of Chowdler's goal. Suddenly, the referee blew his whistle, and when the players separated it was seen that a Chowdlerite was lying disabled on the ground.

'Did you see that?' cried Mr. Chowdler, rushing up to Mr. Black, whom he spied in his neighbourhood.

Mr. Black was a cautious man and shy of committing himself to excitable colleagues, so he replied:

'I was just looking the other way, so I didn't see what happened; but I fear somebody is injured.'

'It was one of the most deliberate and foulest bits of play,' said Mr. Chowdler in a voice for all to hear, 'that I have ever witnessed. Shameful, shameful! From this moment I take no further interest in the game. Good god!' he added suddenly, 'throwing up his hands with a gesture of despair, 'it's Le Willow!' And he hurried off to assist the victim.

Le Willow had sprained an ankle and had to be helped off the field. When he had been removed and the players had resumed their places, it became evident that the referee had awarded a free kick. 'All very well!' muttered Mr. Chowdler to Mr. Rankin, as he hurried back to his post on the touch-line, 'but what's the use of a free kick when it has cost you your best man!'

It was indeed a poor consolation – merely a black mark against an unscrupulous foe who cared nothing for black marks. But imagine Mr. Chowdler's horror, indignation, and dismay when he suddenly realised that the free kick had been awarded, not for, but against his house.

'Monstrous!' he cried aloud, as if appealing to the silent gods. 'Monstrous! I saw the foul, I saw it myself. A perfectly monstrous decision!'

But, monstrous or not, such *was* the decision and there was no appeal from it. There was a moment of intense silence, and then a moan went up from the Trimbleites and a roar of triumph from the Chowdlerites as the shot, which should have equalised, passed just over, instead of under, the bar. For the next twenty minutes the Chowdlerite goal was literally bombarded. Excitement, it is true, made the shooting rather erratic; but, time after time, it looked as if the citadel must fall. And it *would* have fallen, but for Cheeny. When Le Willow received his mortal wound, Cheeny had stepped into his place as leader; and he was everywhere. It is the right thing in the Chiltern game for the leader to be everywhere; that is one of the features that has made of the Chiltern game the great moral training that it is. So Cheeny did his best to be ubiquitous, and played such a game as had not been played in Colonus within the memory of that generation – falling, rising, charging and being charged, stopping rushes, intercepting passes and spoiling shots. And after each unsuccessful attack on the Chowdlerite goal, Mr. Trimble said calmly, 'That settles it! Silly asses! They deserve to be beaten!'

As for Mr. Chowdler, the perspiration stood on his brow and there was a note of almost despairing appeal in his familiar rallying cry, 'Good lads! Good lads all! Stick *to* it, stick *to* it!' But slowly, at the back of his mind, a purpose was shaping itself – a resolve that, if the impossible *did* happen and Cheeny kept the goal intact, then Cheeny should be his Prefect. For a lad with such nerve and courage had proved himself fit to govern, even though he were rather low in the school.

Meanwhile, as the minutes slipped away, the excitement grew and grew, and there was one continuous roar of Chowd*lers*! Jow*lers*! Trim*bulls*! in all keys and every degree of hoarseness. People leapt into the air, slapped each other on the back, threw their caps on to the ground and trampled on them, and performed all manner of strange and inconsequent antics. Ten – eight – six – four minutes more! And then, just at the end, amid howls of delight from their supporters, the defence, with Cheeny at their head, broke away; and, when the whistle blew, the ball was in mid-field and Chowdler's were left victorious by two goals to one.

Mr. Chowdler was swept away by a wave of intense, almost religious, emotion. Foul play, monstrous decisions, past and present wrongs were all forgotten for the moment. If the headmaster had come up and grasped him by the hand, he would have fallen upon the headmaster's neck – he would have fallen upon *anybody's* neck. Never since the relief of Ladysmith, where his own son was beleaguered, had he experienced such a sense of thankfulness, joy, and exultation. Perhaps it was an unconscious association of ideas which made him say to Mr. Tipham as he passed him:

'Thank god! We have kept the flag flying!'

'Where?' asked Mr. Tipham icily.

But already Mr. Chowdler was far away. He had caught sight of Mr. Trimble's retreating figure, and was hurrying after him with the chivalrous intention of pouring balm into smarting wounds. Mr. Trimble was, indeed, making off as fast as he could, in the hope of avoiding an application of this particular balm, which he had sampled on previous occasions and which had always disagreed with him. His nerves were tingling, and he was conscious of a feeling of suppressed irritation which, he knew, would give him a broken night and spoil life for several days. Suddenly, a heavy woollen glove descended on to his shoulder and a manly voice panted in his ear:

'Condolences, poor old boy, condolences! My turn to-day, yours, perhaps, to-morrow!'

'Hullo!' said Mr. Trimble, turning round and shuddering slightly under the caress. 'Is that you, Chowdler? I was looking for you; congratulations.'

'Ta,' said Mr. Chowdler, without removing his hand. 'Ta. We were a bit too good for you, but you put up a tip-top fight. I'm afraid your lot are a bit done up; it always tells hardest on the beaten side. I expect my own lads have had very nearly as much as they wanted. But *what* a game!'

It is much easier to congratulate a successful rival than to receive his condolences gratefully; and Mr. Trimble's vexation pierced through his reply.

'It was indeed,' he replied; 'the worst exhibition I've ever seen in a Cock-house match! On to-day's form any ordinarily respectable side ought to have whopped you, but my lot were simply beneath contempt: they didn't deserve to win. Plenty of spirit, of course; one expects that; but *the* very worst football I've ever seen in Colonus.'

Mr. Chowdler withdrew his hand and the balm with it. As he said afterwards to his wife, poor old Trimble never could take a beating.

To Mr. Chowdler the victory did not mean merely that his boys, by superior luck or skill, had scored one goal more than the boys of another house. It meant, somehow, that the Lanchester tradition had been vindicated; that all that was best and noblest in the place, all that made the past glorious and the present fruitful, had, in the face of tremendous odds, asserted itself in a supreme and convincing manner. He was glad that his house had taken the field with two of their best players away, glad that Le Willow had sprained his ankle and that the referee had been flagrantly unfair. All things had worked together for good, and misfortunes which looked like irretrievable disasters had only served to enhance the moral sublimity of the victory. 'God's in His Heaven, all's right with the world.'

Something of all this Mr. Chowdler certainly said to his house in the speech that he made to them at prayers that evening; and when, on the following day, little Simpkin looked up at him with a wistful smile and said, 'Sir, don't you think that the Lanchester tradition comes out at football?' he felt that the boys had the root of the matter in them too. And he related the story to all his colleagues in turn – and to some of them twice.

Chapter 10

THE LANCHESTER LETTERS

THE term did not end without further unpleasantness. The treatment of Le
Willow had created a feeling of deep resentment in the school, and this
feeling was intensified when Old Chilternians came down and said that
the place was becoming a regular Sunday school, and that the new man
deserved to be shot. It was known, too, that some of the masters shared
the opinion of the Old Chilternians, and 'the Jowler' was generally
recognised as the champion who was foremost in defending the old flag
against attacks. Mr. Chowdler himself was quite unconscious that he had
revealed his inner mind to the boys or fanned the flame of disloyalty. But
there was no doubt that he talked with great freedom to parents and old
boys; and neither parents nor old boys are invariably discreet.

The upshot of it all was that at the school concert on the last night but
one of the term, both Mr. Chowdler and Le Willow received a great
ovation which contrasted forcibly with the very faint cheering that
greeted the entrance of the headmaster. It was said that there had even
been hissing; but while some maintained that it had proceeded from a
group of old boys, and some ascribed it to isolated members of Mr.
Chowdler's house, others asserted that there had been nothing of the kind
at all. Anyhow, it was not very marked, and Mr. Flaggon ignored it. He
had a disconcerting way of concealing his feelings, an air of
impenetrability which suggested, somehow, that he might have a trump
card up his sleeve. The boys did not like him the better for this. Boys feel
more at home with man who plays with all his cards on the table.

But the school got a glimpse into the working of their headmaster's
mind when they were summoned into the Great Hall, just before the last
chapel, to hear some remarks which Mr. Flaggon thought it his duty to
address to them. The term, he said, had been an unsatisfactory term. He
dwelt on the prevalence of cribbing, on the general slackness of discipline

and the apparent absence of any healthy public opinion on matters that were vital to the school. He spoke sternly, but in measured language and without exaggeration or bitterness, and he ended with an appeal to the best traditions of the school and the better instincts of the better boys. There were no threats; but everybody realised that the speech was intended as a grave warning.

Many of the masters were considerably impressed by it. A few of the older ones, however, headed by Mr. Chowdler, chose to regard it as an unwarranted attack on themselves. The boys listened, as boys will always listen to easy and effective speaking, with every appearance of being moved; and the singing in chapel, immediately afterwards, was unusually subdued. But, as soon as the first effect had worn off and the tongues of the scoffers were unloosed, the discontented spirit reasserted itself again, and the opinion most commonly expressed in the houses that night was that they had been treated like preparatory schoolboys. A few there were, chiefly boys in the highest forms, who felt dimly that they had been brought face to face with a real man and a nobler conception of life than they had hitherto realised; but, as yet, they were only few and they held their peace, leaving the talking to the malcontents.

On the first morning of the holidays, the headmaster had a long interview with Mr. Chase. Mr. Chase was not altogether happy about his house; no more was Mr. Flaggon. Indeed, he was not very happy about any of the houses. In his dealings with offenders who had been reported to him in the course of the term, he had been painfully struck by a kind of moral hardness in them, an apparent imperviousness to the influences that make life a noble thing. It stamped itself on their faces in a particular look which was half defiant, half bored, and a sort of easy insolence which seemed to mistake itself for good breeding. And it was something new in his experience. With the thoughtless, dare-devil, and impetuous temperament his own school days had made him familiar; but this was a new type, which seemed incapable of repentance and met punishment and appeal alike with the same callous indifference.

And as he watched the boys' faces day by day and week by week from his place in chapel, he was conscious of a gradual deterioration in many of them. Bigger boys, who at the beginning of the term had suggested, with all their uncouthness, something of the frankness and spontaneity of healthy-minded youth, were growing old and veiled and blasé. Even among the new boys there were some who had exchanged the frank and grubby light-heartedness, natural to their years, for a look of self-conscious pertness that was decidedly unpleasing. It seemed as if there were a blight upon the place, some secret impalpable influence that was poisoning the springs of life. Mr. Flaggon had diagnosed it at first as a lack of discipline, and he had set himself to fight the evil with heroic remedies. Cost what it might, he would have discipline. But he was beginning to suspect that indiscipline was only a symptom and that he had not yet penetrated to the root of the mischief.

By his advice Mr. Chase, who was conscientious if unimaginative, was getting rid of some of the older boys in his house, who had been vegetating for a long time in the lower forms. He now suggested that the house-master should try to establish confidential relations with some of the parents of his new boys, and find out from them, if possible, whether all was really well. Mr. Chase looked dubious. 'I don't quite like it,' he said. 'It seems a little underhand – rather like going behind people's backs; because I have been talking a good deal lately to my Prætor and to some of the old boys, and they all assure me that, though there is a prejudice in the school against my house, it is really quite right and as good as any. Besides, I don't want to alarm parents unnecessarily.'

Mr. Flaggon concealed a slight feeling of impatience. 'We mustn't,' he said, 'allow ourselves to be bound by a more than Spanish etiquette. We have got to do the very best we can for the boys who are under us, and if we don't use whatever help the parents can give us, we are surely guilty of a grave breach of duty. And as for frightening them – no sensible parent would be alarmed at being asked to co-operate with us in the interests of his child. Only, you must choose the right parents; for I'm really afraid there are some who don't mind what happens to their sons, provided they do well at their games and have a good time.'

Mr. Chase yielded to persuasion, and, when he had gone, Mr. Flaggon sat down to a still harder task. He had decided that he must write to Mr. Chowdler. Ordinarily, in handling a delicate situation, he preferred the spoken to the written word. But in this case he felt that he could write more calmly and sympathetically than he could speak; for he was conscious that Mr. Chowdler's voice and personality jarred upon him, and he feared that, in an interview, this latent irritation might betray itself in a tone or a gesture which would embitter rather than end the quarrel. Anyhow, something had to be done, for the situation was rapidly becoming impossible. Mr. Flaggon was aware of Mr. Chowdler's indiscretions. The knowledge had come to him through various channels; and once or twice lately, Mr. Chowdler's tone and language to himself had been of a kind which it is difficult for a headmaster to ignore with dignity.

The letter was a difficult one to compose, and Mr. Flaggon weighed his words very carefully. He tried to recall Mr. Chowdler to a sense of elementary loyalty. He had, he said, every respect for differences of opinion, and he did not expect his own views or actions to pass uncriticised. But there were limits to the manner in which such criticisms could be expressed without doing harm to the school, and he was bound to say that, on several occasions, Mr. Chowdler had – quite unconsciously, no doubt – gone beyond those limits. He disclaimed any personal animus, and ended with a generous tribute to Mr. Chowdler's many services to Chiltern.

When he had read and re-read the letter and marked it 'private', he dispatched it by a messenger and anxiously awaited the reply.

And he did not have long to wait. Whenever his indiscretions were called in question, Mr. Chowdler made great play with the word 'gossip.' The headmaster, said Mr. Chowdler, had evidently been listening to gossip, and would do well to be more shy of it in the future. He (Mr. Chowdler) had nothing to reproach himself with, and he refused to be held responsible for other folk's mistakes. His advice had always been at the service of the headmaster, but it had been consistently ignored. People must lie in their beds as they make them.

The headmaster sighed as he read this answer to his appeal, but he felt that nothing would be gained by continuing the correspondence or dotting the 'i's'. He hoped against hope that, though Mr. Chowdler was incapable of admitting himself to be in the wrong, he would lay the admonition to heart and be more cautious in the future.

Mr. Flaggon spent the greater part of the holidays at Chiltern, working at a rough draft of a new curriculum and mastering a great mass of detail. It was rumoured that his mother and sister were coming to live with him in the summer; but at present they were wintering abroad, and Mr. Flaggon was alone. In the course of the holidays he became more closely acquainted with Mr. Bent. The two men, each out for a solitary walk, had come from opposite footpaths into the same lane. Neither was in search of company, but, as both were obviously bound in the same direction, escape was impossible.

'Hullo!' said Mr. Flaggon. 'I didn't know you were here still, Bent. I thought you were sure to be in Switzerland.'

'No,' said Mr. Bent; 'I have shed my youthful indiscretions. I still can't stand Chiltern in the Easter or summer holidays, but I have at last realised, with infinite relief, that at Christmas no place is so attractive as one's own fireside. It saves me a world of anxious thought and planning. I just run up to town for the last week-end, and that gives me the feeling, necessary to the pedagogue, of having been away and seen things.'

Mr. Flaggon had not had time or opportunity to become at all intimate with any of his staff. He was, as we have said, by nature rather shy and reticent, and the consciousness of much latent hostility had made advances unusually difficult. There had, of course, been formal calls and dinner-parties; but neither calls nor dinner-parties lend themselves to the formation of friendships.

Mr. Bent had been a puzzle to him. The flippancy of his tone and manner at masters' meetings had often been annoying; but he had sometimes said things which suggested ideals and a breadth of view at variance with his apparent cynicism. When, therefore, as they were passing his house, Mr. Bent said, 'Won't you come in and have a cup of tea?' Mr. Flaggon accepted the invitation. That walk and tea led to other walks and other teas. Mr. Bent recognised in the headmaster a man of great mental alertness and wide interests; and Mr. Flaggon discovered an unexpectedly serious vein in his companion, veiled, as it often was, under an ironic humour. As conversation became more intimate, Mr. Bent ventured one day to express his inner feelings about Chiltern and the Lanchester tradition.

'We are haunted here,' he said, 'as you have doubtless observed, by the ghost of greatness; and it won't let us speak, or think, or do. Nothing is so paralysing (the preachers call it inspiring) as the memory of a great man. If I want a new Latin prose book, I can't have it because Dr. Lanchester taught out of the old one; and if I want a window that will open, it is impossible because Lanchester didn't believe in ventilation. This, of course, is fearful heresy, and men have died on the scaffold for less.'

'I'm sorry,' said Mr. Flaggon with a laugh, 'that you are so prejudiced against Lanchester, because I had a proposal to make to you. I've just come into possession of some papers of his, and I was going to ask you to look through them for me and see if they contain anything of real interest. I simply haven't got time myself.'

'Oh, of course, I wasn't crabbing the *real* Lanchester,' said Mr. Bent; 'it's only his ghost that annoys me. The *man* was an educational reformer, but the *ghost* is only a glorified cricket "pro." What are the papers?'

'They have been sent me,' replied the headmaster, 'by a Mrs. Core, whose grandfather wrote the life of Dr. Lanchester. Probably the best things are in the book already, but there may be a gem here and there that has been passed over. Would you care to do a little sifting?'

'I should love it,' said Mr. Bent. 'You see, we have done what the descendants of prophet-slayers always do. We have hidden away *our* prophet under a showy tomb, built out of the very stones that slew him. I should vastly enjoy digging for his bones.'

So Mr. Bent carried home, one day, a boxful of old papers, and spent several happy evenings going over them. The gem of the collection was a little bundle of letters, writing to an intimate friend during the early years of the doctor's headmastership, and so outspoken in their comments on persons and events that, apparently, the biographer had been afraid to use them. Such phrases as 'I am determined, God willing, to lift this school out of the mire into which it has fallen. . . The unruly spirit of the boys troubles me less than the prejudice of the masters. . . Alexander the coppersmith' (probably an allusion to the Rev. John Alexander, at that time second master at Chiltern) 'does me much harm. . . I apprehend more and more clearly that a headmaster must be a despot. . . . The moral and intellectual deadness of these people to the larger issues of education appals me' – delighted Mr. Bent and whetted his appetite for more. When he returned the papers at the end of the week, he observed:

'There's matter enough here to blow up Chiltern and half the county into the bargain. Some of the letters are splendid and quite new, but it would never do to publish them. People would say they were an impudent forgery. Lanchester was a much finer fellow than I realised, and intensely modern. By the way, I understood he had had difficulties, but I never knew that he had to begin by sacking a third of the school and two of the senior—' But a look on Mr. Flaggon's face pulled him up abruptly. 'That's the worst of headmasters,' he said to himself afterwards. 'The moment you begin to be natural with them, you tumble up against the official.

But Mr. Flaggon was not offended. He had merely remembered, suddenly and with a twinge of pain, the difficult problems that confronted him, and what sharp remedies he might be forced to employ before they were finally solved.

Chapter 11

MR. CHOWDLER WINS A BATTLE AND
MEETS WITH A REBUFF

WHEN term began again towards the end of January, Mr. Tipham and his many-coloured scarf were no longer a feature of Chiltern. He had transferred himself to Cambridge and tutorial work, feeling possibly that Cleopas College and the undergraduate were in closer touch with Nature than Chiltern and the public schoolboy. Anyhow he was gone, and his place had been taken by a young man of less pronounced views, who wore spectacles and listened deferentially to Mr. Chowdler.

Mr. Chowdler himself had returned in splendid fighting form. He had spent the greater part of the holidays at Sauersprudel, and he had employed the time in wrestling and prevailing. Long before 'all the vulgar people that Harry hates so' (we are quoting from Mrs. Chowdler) flocked out to Switzerland at Christmas, Mr. Chowdler had discovered Sauersprudel in the Spitzenthal and planted the British flag there. It is true that all the English families who have visited the place in Mr. Chowdler's wake speak of themselves as having discovered it too. But that does not alter the fact that Mr. Chowdler was the real Christopher Columbus of Sauersprudel and the father of the Adler Hotel – at least as a winter resort.

In the early days of the British occupation the settlers were not numerous, but they came regularly every winter. There were, besides Mr. and Mrs. Chowdler, the Hon. Fitzroy Plashy and party, Canon and Mrs. Dubbin, Dr. Cushat and family, Mr. Weatherbury, K.C., and a few others who had suddenly realised that sunshine and frost are not peculiar to the Engadine, and that Sauersprudel is much nearer to London than St. Moritz is. These pioneers lived together on fairly amicable terms, enjoying equal rights, but possessing no written laws, no organised constitution.

But, as the tide of cheap immigration brought strange faces to the Adlerhof in ever increasing numbers, the old patriarchal life was bound to come to an end in favour of some system more congenial to the British temperament – one, that is to say, which would classify the guests and admit of a distinction between governors and governed. Accordingly, Mr. Chowdler and the original families took up the white man's burden, formed themselves into a permanent committee, and set themselves to organise life on the principles which have made sport the thing it is. They created a skating club, a tobogganing club, a ski-ing club, and a curling club, each with rules and tests and an etiquette of its own; they appointed competitions, and decided in what particular form of dissipation the guests were to indulge of an evening. In a word, they gave the Adlerhof the blessings of a firm and orderly government. With a prescriptive right to the best rooms and the chief place at feasts, they were the aristocracy of the hotel, governing, as befits an aristocracy, in the interests of the many, but holding discreetly aloof.

Unfortunately, amongst Britons, one of the first results of a firm government is a factious and discontented Opposition; and the Adlerhof was no exception to the rule. No sooner had Mr. Chowdler and his friends assumed the cares of office than murmurs of complaint began to be heard, feeble at first but gathering strength with each successive season. Wild young men and women, athirst for bandy and bunny-hugs, for impossible ski-jumps and noisy races along the corridors, protested that they had not come out to be drilled like schoolboys but to enjoy themselves; and they began to question the authority of the self-appointed committee. Profoundly ignorant of the past history of the place and of all that it owed to its aristocracy, they felt no reverence for Mr. Chowdler and the Hon. Fitzroy Plashy circling sedately round an orange, and only wondered why the best part of the rink was reserved for these old fogeys and their friends. At last a moment came when, conscious of their strength, they passed from murmurs to action. When the committee arranged a toboggan race, the opposition organised a ski-ing competition; when the committee decreed a gymkhana, the opposition engineered a dance; and the hotel was divided into hostile camps.

Things were in this critical state when, on December 28, Mr. Chowdler arrived in Sauersprudel to lend his powerful support to the cause of law and order. His annual appearance had always been treated as an event of importance in the life of the hotel – obsequious smiles from mine host and a flutter among the servants. You would have thought him a governor returning to his colony, or a chieftain to his clan. But, on this occasion, Mr. Chowdler, who had left his wife at home, was met in the hall by the landlord with a face of woe. The room on the first floor with the south aspect, the room that he had selected as his own in 1896 and which had been specially reserved for him ever since, had been forcibly annexed and occupied, a fortnight previously, by a young English Herr who refused to turn out for all the Chowdlers in creation. Would Mr. Chowdler mind going into a room on the other side of the passage for a few days – a larger and a better room, though facing north? The young Herr talked of leaving very shortly.

'His name?' asked Mr. Chowdler curtly.

'Mr. Maurice Veal of London.'

'Bring him to me,' said Mr. Chowdler.

Impossible; the young man had gone out ski-ing for the day, taking his lunch with him.

'Then send my boxes up to my room,' said Mr. Chowdler. 'My *own* room, mind. I will arrange matters.'

The landlord hesitated between fear of Mr. Chowdler and the danger of losing a wealthy customer who drank champagne every night and paid exactly twice as much for the room as Mr. Chowdler did. But fear of Mr. Chowdler prevailed; and when young Mr. Veal returned from his day's sport at five in the afternoon, he found his own effects in the passage and Mr. Chowdler, in shirt sleeves, busily engaged in installing himself in the disputed apartment.

Mr. Veal, though not deficient in bounce, was not remarkable for his physical proportions. Perhaps a long and fatiguing day in the snow, in the course of which he had taken many severe falls, had damped his spirits; or, perhaps, the sight of Mr. Chowdler in shirt sleeves, with his broad shoulders, bullet head, red face, and determined jaw, was more formidable than anything he had anticipated. At all events he lost his nerve, and, after a little bluster and some futile threats, he withdrew to abuse the landlord, leaving Mr. Chowdler in possession.

'I engaged this room in 1896,' Mr. Chowdler shouted after him, 'and I intend to keep it.'

And he kept it.

However, the victory of the bedroom did not end the campaign against the committee; it only spurred the enemy to greater exertions. And young Veal, panting for revenge, became the recognised leader of a guerrilla campaign. No step that the committee took was allowed to pass unchallenged; no rule was made but it was straightaway broken, no notice was posted without provoking a counter-notice or a parody. Half the hotel was on terms of active hostility with the other half. The older men and their wives stood by the committee, the younger ones rallied round the banner of Veal. And a climax seemed to have been reached one afternoon, when Veal and a friend dashed across the sacred enclosure, where Messrs. Chowdler, Plashy and Weatherbury were cutting figures, kicked away the orange which formed the centre of their evolutions, and spilled Mr.

Chowdler – accidentally, as they maintained; of set purpose and malice aforethought, as others asserted. After this anything was possible. But the situation was saved by the timely arrival of Lord Budleigh of Salterton and his brother the Admiral. By a masterly stroke of policy they were co-opted on to the committee before they had been five minutes in the hotel; and the opposition collapsed. For even in moments of the wildest aberration, a hotelful of English folks knows the value of a lord. Moreover, Lord Budleigh was a man of courteous and conciliatory manners, far less exclusive in his behaviour than either Mr. Chowdler or the Hon. Fitzroy Plashy, and tolerant of the vagaries of youth; while his brother the Admiral, who was out to enjoy himself and sublimely unconscious of anything amiss, fraternised with everybody in the most natural and friendly way. Within eight-and-forty hours, Mr. Veal found himself without followers and left the hotel. The committee had triumphed, and, with the committee, Mr. Chowdler.

'There *had* been a little unpleasantness before I arrived,' he said afterwards, in describing the events, 'but I soon settled all that.'

It will be readily understood, therefore, that Mr. Chowdler was in no mood to tolerate rebuffs when he returned to Chiltern. And yet, as ill-luck would have it, a rebuff of the most unexpected kind awaited him. On the eve of his departure for Switzerland he had written to the headmaster to intimate that he wished to have Cheeny as a house Prefect in the following term, and it would therefore be convenient if the boy were made a school Prefect at the same time. In all his past experience a wish of this kind had been equivalent to a command, and had only needed the official endorsement of the headmaster. However, this time, on his return from Sauersprudel, he found, not the official endorsement he expected, but a note, requesting him to come and see Mr. Flaggon on the matter at his earliest convenience. The interview was more surprising even than the note. Mr. Flaggon, it appeared, intended, when appointing Prefects, to take much less account in future of mere athletic distinction and much more of mental ability; 'because,' he said, 'although I know that there are often striking exceptions, brain power and character are closely allied, and the boy who has brains is more likely to understand and appreciate high ideals than the boy who has none. I have gone into Cheeny's claims very carefully; and, except for your high opinion of him, which of course weighs with me, I can find no reason for promoting him to such a responsible post. He is quite low in the school and—'

'Then you can't have seen him in the Cock-house match last term,' interrupted Mr. Chowdler angrily.

'I did,' replied Mr. Flaggon, 'I admired his spirit and I envied him his agility. But that kind of spirit alone doesn't make a Prefect; and I notice that all his masters say of him that he collapses before any difficulty in his work and is inclined to sulk.'

Mr. Chowdler was too indignant to speak; but worse was in store; for Mr. Flaggon continued implacably:

'But there is another boy in your house whom I *am* very glad to make a Prefect. I mean Dennison. He has earned the honour by his place in the school alone, and, so far as I can judge – and I have been studying him rather closely – he has qualities which justify me in feeling very hopeful about him.'

Dennison! Mr. Chowdler nearly had a fit. Dennison! One of those morbid, cantankerous, precocious boys, who have none of the good-fellowship, none of the joy of life, that are the crown of youth. A boy with a jealous, sour, carping disposition, unpopular with his fellows and unresponsive to his house-master; a boy without influence and eaten up by an unhealthy egotism.

'You misjudge him,' said Mr. Flaggon. 'The boy is reserved, rather sensitive, and shy of expressing himself; but he has character and a conscience. With guidance and a little sympathy he will make a very useful Prefect.'

'*Will* make!' Mr. Chowdler protested vehemently. *He* knew the boy as only a house-master *could* know a boy, whereas the headmaster was only judging superficially. At no price would he accept Dennison as a Prefect in his house.

'I am sorry,' said Mr. Flaggon stiffly, 'to be obliged to force on you as Prefect a boy with whom you are clearly so much out of sympathy. But I have quite made up my mind to make Dennison a school Prefect;

and, of course, if he is a school Prefect, he must be a house Prefect too.'

'In that case,' said Mr. Chowdler, scarlet with passion, 'I decline to be responsible for anything that may happen in my house.'

'Those are serious words for a house-master to use,' said Mr. Flaggon gravely.

'They were not spoken in jest,' retorted Mr. Chowdler, as he left the study; and, though the headmaster made no reply, he realised that things could not go on much longer on this unsatisfactory footing.

From that moment Mr. Chowdler became a man with an obsession. The mere mention of the name Flaggon temporarily upset his mental balance. In all the petty annoyances of life he saw the hand of Flaggon, and anybody who was not ready to curse Flaggon by all his gods became at once suspect.

At Chiltern, as in all intellectual societies, the personal doings and idiosyncrasies of its individual members formed the staple of daily conversation; and before the term was two days old, Mr. Chowdler knew that Bent and Flaggon had walked together in the holidays, taken tea together, and, no doubt, conspired together. He never *had* liked Bent – a cynical egotist (all the people whom Mr. Chowdler disliked were egotists) with dangerous principles. He shouldn't wonder if Bent had been poisoning the 'empty one's' mind against Cheeny. Bent always had a grudge against *his* boys.

Accordingly, coming across Bent one morning in the masters' reading-room, which adjoined the Common Room, he could not resist the impulse to attack.

'Well, Bent,' he said, in tones of forced geniality through which the sarcasm pierced like a needle, 'I'm told I ought to congratulate you on your promotion. I hear that you have been privileged to drink deep draughts out of the Flaggon in the holidays. I hope you found the beverage stimulating.'

Mr. Bent had returned from his week-end in town with a chill on the liver which made him disagreeable to his friends and offensive to his foes. He flushed with anger, but forced himself to reply with affected airiness.

'Very, thank you. And I suppose you have been rapping tables and communicating with the spook of old Lanchester. Did he tell you, by the way, that I have been reading some unpublished letters of his, which are rather sensational and upset most of your pet theories about the tradition?'

It came as a perpetual surprise to Mr. Chowdler, whenever they had words, that Bent did not know how to behave like a gentleman or answer a civil question civilly. But this went beyond all bounds. So he drew himself up and replied with dignity:

'I am not in the habit of answering flippant and offensive questions.'

'In that case,' said Mr. Bent, suddenly losing his self-control, 'I should advise you not to make offensive and impertinent remarks about matters which don't concern you.'

Which reply left Mr. Chowdler justly indignant, and confirmed him in the belief that Bent *had* had something to do with the rejection of Cheeny.

Chapter 12

THE EXPLOSION

OTHER people than Mr. Chowdler were dissatisfied with the state of affairs, though none expressed disapproval with quite such acrimony. For the first time for many years the numbers in the school were down. This was in part due to the deliberate action of the headmaster. Veterans in the lower forms of the school had been invited to 'move on'; and the veterans were numerous. But there was another reason for the shrinkage and one on which Mr. Chowdler and his friends were more inclined to lay stress; namely, that several names had been withdrawn at the eleventh hour from the January entrance list. From the nature of its clientèle, Chiltern was affected, more than most schools, by the gossip of the London clubs; and, in the London clubs, opinion was not favourable to the new régime. The case of Le Willow had created a most unfortunate impression. '*I'm* not going to send my boy to a school where they sack for cribbing,' said one parent to another. 'Cribbed myself when I was a boy, and so did all my pals.'

'The new man's no sportsman,' added a second, 'and the boys simply can't stick him.'

'No more can the masters,' interjected a third. 'I met one of them in Switzerland, and, from what *he* said, I should say the place was simply going to pot as fast as it can.'

In Mr. Chowdler's eyes the place undoubtedly was 'going to pot.' In season and out of season he called everybody's attention to this lamentable truth, and the fact that he was unable to prevent it preyed upon his mind. It preyed to such an extent that a moment came when he committed an act which brought on the inevitable crisis.

In the third week of term the headmaster convened a special masters' meeting to discuss certain matters which he considered urgent. Not only did he convene it for the particular time at which Mr. Chowdler was accustomed to play a round of golf, but the first item on the programme was the question of Sunday hours.

Now the Sunday arrangements at Chiltern were perhaps unusual, but they were hallowed by tradition and shared, in a way, the sacred character of the day. Briefly, they left a clear break, interrupted only by tea, between lunch at 1.30 and chapel at eight. Exact contemporaries of Mr. Chowdler might have recalled that, in his early days, he himself had viewed this long interval with disfavour. But it is no reproach to a man to change his mind, and, with a riper experience, Mr. Chowdler had learned to love and value the Chiltern Sunday. To himself it meant a long country walk and a most refreshing snooze afterwards; but that was not the reason why he valued it. He valued it because it was so good for the boys; because it gave them, what no other school gives its boys, time to know themselves, time for thought, and especially *home* thoughts; and because it made of Sunday what Sunday ought to be, 'a morally recuperative day.' 'We must put our foot down,' he said to his colleagues; 'there must be no tampering with Sunday.'

Masters' meetings at Chiltern were held in the library. The headmaster and the ten house-masters sat round an oak table; the others occupied chairs wherever chairs happened to be. This disposition of forces created a rather invidious distinction between the juniors and the ten who often abused their position to make important remarks in tones which were inaudible to the rest of the meeting. But the invidiousness was felt more keenly by the juniors than by the ten. Mr. Flaggon disliked the arrangement for other reasons. Seated at the head of the table, *primus inter pares*, he felt uncomfortably close to the house-masters and inconveniently removed from the rest of the staff; and, if he wished to be heard by all, he had to raise his voice and speak through, or over, his immediate neighbours in a way that was unpleasant for both. He sighed for a dais and a more elevated seat, and accordingly he had suggested tentatively to some of the senior men the advisability of holding the meetings elsewhere. But the suggestion had given genuine pain. It was unthinkable that Chiltern masters should meet anywhere but under the portrait of Dr. Lanchester; and the only other portrait of Dr. Lanchester was in the Great Hall, an obviously impossible place. So, wishing to avoid unnecessary friction, Mr. Flaggon had resigned himself to the library for the present. Perhaps, as he sat with his back to the portrait, he was less conscious of inspiration than his colleagues.

It was therefore from the traditional place, at the head of the oak table, that Mr. Flaggon made the remarks which provoked a scene memorable in the annals of Chiltern. It had been borne in upon him, he said, by events in the preceding term, that the long interval between dinner and chapel was fraught with considerable danger. The danger was obviously greater in the summer term than in any other, when lock-up was later; and, some time in March, he proposed to consider a complete rearrangement of the time-table for the day. But, for the present, he wished to make as little change as possible. He was therefore going to ask house-masters to arrange for a preparation in their houses at half-past four on Sundays. Tea would be at 5.30 and chapel at the usual time.

Mr. Chowdler had come to the meeting in the worst of tempers. Apart from the fact that he was deeply attached to the *status quo*, he had been deprived of his golf, and being a man of full habit of body, he could not afford to miss his exercise. And so the headmaster had scarcely finished speaking, when he broke in with no attempt to conceal his anger.

'It has always been customary,' he said, 'to consult house-masters on matters of this kind before raising them at a general meeting.'

Mr. Flaggon lifted his eyebrows slightly, but replied quite calmly: 'I shall be glad to consider any difficulties that may be put to me in private; but in a matter of this kind, on which I feel very strongly, I must decide for myself and in accordance with my own judgment.'

'Do I understand,' cried Mr. Chowdler, raising his voice and glaring at his chief, 'that we are to have this ill-considered ukase thrust down our throats without discussion? Because, if so, let me say that this is an indignity to which we are *not* accustomed.'

'I think I have made it clear,' said Mr. Flaggon, 'that I do not propose to take a vote on this question, and I have stated my reasons; I wish to see the experiment tried.'

'In that case,' said Mr. Chowdler, turning half round in his chair so as to face his colleagues, 'I, for one, shall decline to obey.'

'I have noted your refusal with extreme regret,' replied Mr. Flaggon, so quietly that the words would hardly have been heard in the more distant parts of the room, if it had not been for the intense silence that prevailed. And then, before anybody had recovered from the surprise and shock, he passed on to the second item on the programme.

The rest of the business was dispatched rapidly and without any of the irrelevant comment which was usually a feature of masters' meetings. Everybody was anxious to get away, to breathe the fresh air, and to take stock of his own and other people's impressions.

'Chowdler's downed him,' whispered Mr. Rankin, as the masters trooped into the great quadrangle with grave and anxious faces.

'I don't know,' replied the younger man thus addressed. 'It can't end there. And,' he added, it *ought* not to end there.'

Whether Mr. Chowdler felt any secret misgivings, it is impossible to say. Probably not. By dint of always speaking of 'the empty one' he had persuaded himself that Mr. Flaggon was essentially a weak, unmeritable man who was aping the despot. Besides, Mr. Chowdler was not an adept at self-criticism, and was quite incapable of looking at himself from the outside. Presumably, therefore, he regarded his display of temper as an outburst of passionate but righteous indignation, a kind of prophetic 'Thus saith the Lord.' And as the day ended without further incident, he may have thought, with Mr. Rankin, that the man Flaggon was 'downed.'

But, on the morrow, two things happened which brought him face to face with some very unpleasant facts. At first lesson a notice came round to say that in future, on Sunday afternoons, there would be preparation in houses at 4.30 o'clock; and later on in the morning he received a letter from the headmaster couched in the following terms:

DEAR MR. CHOWDLER,

I have put off writing till to-day in the hope that some word from you would enable me to take a course different from the one which the events of yesterday and your subsequent silence compel me to pursue. I hope that I shall never fear honest and outspoken criticism. But there are decencies to be observed without which a headmaster's position becomes impossible; and your behaviour to myself yesterday leaves me no alternative but to assume that you intended deliberately to challenge my authority as headmaster. It is with a grave sense of responsibility and in no vindictive spirit that I feel obliged to request you to send in your resignation, to take effect at the end of the present term.

Yours faithfully,
S. E. FLAGGON.

The first effect of this letter on Mr. Chowdler was to make him feel as if the solid ground were crumbling away beneath him; but the next moment his combative spirit reasserted itself and, dashing to his writing-table, he scribbled off what he afterwards described as 'a calm and dignified reply.'

SIR,

      I think we may speak to each other in plain English. What you are pleased to call a request for my resignation, *I* call a notice of dismissal. I shall therefore exercise my right of appeal (see 'Statutes,' p. 131, Schedule D, Clause 4.) The Council must decide between us.

Yours, etc.,

H. CHOWDLER.

Mr. Flaggon verified the reference and found that, by an old and unrepealed regulation, Mr. Chowdler had indeed the right of appeal to the Council against dismissal. He therefore sent the following note:

DEAR MR. CHOWDLER:

      I am informing the Chairman of the Council of my decision and of the reasons which have dictated it, by to-morrow evening's post at latest. You must take whatever steps you think right.

Yours faithfully,

S. E. FLAGGON.

    The fat, as at least half-a-dozen people said spontaneously, was in the fire, and Chiltern could think and talk of nothing else. There was a general agreement that Chowdler's behaviour at the meeting had passed the limits of decorum; but while the seniors maintained that the headmaster should have ignored the offence in a man whose services to the school were so notorious and of such long standing, many of the juniors held that, if Flaggon didn't give old Chowdler the boot, he was done for. There was an equal difference of opinion as to the probable issue of the appeal. The moderates thought that there was still room for compromise. Chowdler could withdraw his offensive remarks and then Flaggon could withdraw his notice of dismissal. Others, who knew Chowdler's love of battle, were sure that he would fight it out to the end and win. Others, again, did not see how the Council could possibly throw over a headmaster whom they had so recently appointed.

To Mr. Plummer the whole episode as painful in the extreme, and the ideal of a united staff seemed farther off than ever. He was torn between two conflicting loyalties – loyalty to an official chief, and loyalty to a senior colleague. He expressed his inner feelings to Mr. Bent on one of their frequent walks, more from force of habit than because he expected to find a sympathetic listener.

'Of course,' he said, 'one can't defend the way Chowdler *does* things; and nothing could possibly have been worse than his behaviour the other day. Still, one must remember that he has had great provocation – *great* provocation.'

'That's just like you!' replied Mr. Bent. 'Chowdler is for ever trailing his coat across the green, and when he succeeds in tripping somebody, you say that he has had great provocation. What provocation, pray! Name!'

'Well,' said Mr. Plummer, 'there was the Le Willow business to begin with.'

'A matter of principle,' said Mr. Bent. 'A headmaster who sacrificed his principles to a Chowdler, wouldn't be fit to be a crossing-sweeper!'

'And then there was his refusal to make Cheeny Prefect,' said Mr. Plummer doggedly.

'Again a question of principle!' cried his companion. 'And you're talking as if Chowdler were the captain of the ship and Flaggon his second mate.'

'No, I'm not,' said Mr. Plummer. 'But after Gussy, Chowdler's position under a new man was bound to be difficult, and Flaggon ought to have made allowances; he ought to have been more tactful.'

'Tact on Chowdler,' said Mr. Bent, 'is like a feather on a hippopotamus. Chowdler doesn't ask for tact; he demands unconditional surrender.'

'Anyhow,' persisted Mr. Plummer, 'though he does it badly, Chowdler represents what many, if not most, of us feel. You know I'm not one of the people who go shouting their criticisms on the house-tops: but, candidly, I don't approve of the new régime.'

'What don't you approve of, pray?' asked Mr. Bent scornfully. 'The weeding out of the old and incompetent? the attempt to restore discipline? the—'

'I'm not going to particularise,' said Mr. Plummer, 'but I distrust Flaggon's whole attitude; especially in a man who has no experience. The boys are discontented, the staff is divided, the numbers are down, and we're all wondering where it's going to end.'

' "Ye fools and uncircumcised in heart and mind," ' burst out Mr. Bent, ' "ye do always resist the Holy Ghost: as your fathers did, so do ye." '

'That's blasphemous,' cried Mr. Plummer.

'I believe that's what they said of Stephen,' replied Mr. Bent, recovering his composure. 'But, as a matter of fact, I was quoting from an unpublished letter of Lanchester's; and he happened to be speaking of an eighteenth century Chowdler.'

Chapter 13

IN DARK PLACES

IT was obviously to the interest of all parties that the appeal should be settled as soon as possible. But the Council showed no haste in coming to a decision. The delay was ominous, for it seemed to indicate that they regarded the question as an open one.

This being so, Mr. Pounderly and several of his senior colleagues were anxious that the staff should take combined action. There was no doubt in Mr. Pounderly's mind as to what form the combined action should take. 'If,' he said, 'the policy of cutting off the heads of the tallest lilies receives official sanction, it will not stop with Chowdler. The lives and fortunes of all of us are at stake. It is most important that at this crisis the staff should show a united front.'

It took many hours of patient argument to persuade Mr. Pounderly that the front of the staff was not, and could not be, united; and when the unpalatable truth was at last forced in upon him, he went about his daily duties once more wringing his hands and whispering, 'lamentable, lamentable.'

However, he was to have an opportunity of expressing his own views fully and in an influential quarter. Mr. Benison-Benison, a local magnate and a member of the Council, had determined to get to the bottom of things for himself. Mr. Benison-Benison was one of those honest and incapable men whom the British public delights to honour, and his idea of getting to the bottom of things was to give an impartial hearing to one side only. It was the method he had always adopted in forming his opinions on political or theological questions; and he prided himself on his freedom from prejudice. 'I always make a point of studying any controversial topic,' he would say, 'before I make up my mind about it.' Consequently, when he set to work to master the Chiltern problem, he could think of no better way of doing so than by interviewing personally Mr. Chowdler and his friends. At much physical inconvenience to himself, for he was crippled at the moment by rheumatism, he drove over to Chiltern, had a long talk with Mr. Chowdler, and, at that gentleman's suggestion, had separate interviews also with Mr. Pounderly, Mr. Black, Mr. Beadle, and some others of the faction. And, as a result of it all, he carried away 'a very strong impression' that Mr. Chowdler stood for the best interests of the school, that Mr. Flaggon was the wrong man in the wrong place, and that the masters, as a body, would be very glad to see the last of him. And this impression received a striking corroboration from an entirely unprejudiced quarter. Mr. Benison-Benison had occasion to call, on his return journey, at Thrale's, the local motor and motor-cycle shop; and, in answer to some discreet feelers, Mr. Thrale became voluble and stated confidently that Mr. Flaggon was letting down the school 'terrible' and ruining the town, and that the citizens looked confidently to the Council to set matters straight over 'this here appeal they talk of.'

But while the issue was still in doubt and Chiltern was humming with excited gossip, events occurred which turned all thoughts for the moment into other channels.

Mr. Chase, acting on the advice of the headmaster, had written in December to the parents of three of his new boys, asking them to find out, in the course of the holidays, whether the moral tone of the house was in a healthy condition; and if anything was wrong, to communicate confidentially with him. In each case he had received a formal acknowledgement of his letter, and as nothing further had come of it, his mind was at ease. And then, suddenly, a bolt fell from the blue. Mr. Chase received one morning an eight-page letter, marked private and confidential, which made him turn very pale and entirely took away his appetite for breakfast. The writer of this letter related that he had, during the holidays, put certain questions to his son, and after some pressing had extracted from him a story which showed that, from the moral point of view, the school generally and Mr. Chase's house in particular were in a very bad state. The boy, however, had implored him not to say anything to the authorities, as the two worst offenders had left at Christmas and things were certain to be much better next term. He had, however, by that morning's post, received a letter from his boy, which revived all his anxieties. The boy wrote that he was very unhappy and wanted to be taken away. 'Under these circumstances,' the father concluded, 'I feel bound, in the interests of the school as well as of my own child, to take you into my confidence; and I have written you a full account of all that I know. I only beg that, in whatever steps you take, you will manage to keep my boy's name out of it. Dislike of being an informer, and fear of the possible consequences to himself, naturally weigh very heavily on him. But, clearly, something must be done, and done at once; and if you wish it I am quite prepared to come to Chiltern myself and see you about the matter.'

Mr. Chase read the letter several times with a strong sensation of physical nausea, and sat for while afterwards in his study trying to think. When the first shock had passed off, he began to cherish a hope that the boy might perhaps have exaggerated. Now that he came to think of it, it struck him that the boy *was* rather an excitable boy and, very likely, inclined to be hysterical. But he was an honourable man; and though the facts as related were a reflection on his own competence, he carried the letter straight to the headmaster.

Mr. Flaggon guessed what must be passing in his colleague's mind, and his manner was both sympathetic and cordial. He thanked Mr. Chase warmly for having taken him at once into his confidence; and together the two men discussed what ought to be done. Should the father be invited to come to Chiltern and procure further and yet more detailed information, or should they act at once? Mr. Flaggon thought that there was danger in delay. The boy might become frightened and retract or, possibly, give a hint of what was brewing to a friend. 'Our best chance,' he said, 'of getting at the whole truth is to strike at once while the offenders are off their guard; and if the facts are as they have been stated, we have enough to go upon. Besides, if the father comes down and sees his son, everybody will guess the source of our information; and we are bound in honour to keep the boy's secret.' Mr. Chase agreed; and accordingly that evening after locking up, the headmaster went to Mr. Chase's house and held a searching inquiry. Before it was over, he knew a great many things that he had not known before, and realised how very vile, under its deceptive light-heartedness, life can be in a bad house in a bad school.

Next morning, at first lesson, a rumour spread through a startled school that three of the most prominent Chaseites had been summarily expelled, and that others were to leave at the end of the term: and Mr. Chase, who looked as though all joy had gone out of life, confirmed the news to his colleagues. Mr. Flaggon had determined to address the school that evening after chapel; but, before he could do so, fresh developments occurred which decided him to wait a little longer. For in the course of the day, Dennison, the newly appointed Prefect, appeared in his study with a pale face and twitching hands, and asked if he might speak confidentially. The permission was readily granted, and Dennison proceeded to unburden his soul. Everybody, he said, had known for a long time that Chase's house was 'rotten,' but he was afraid his own house was not much better. Since he had been Prefect, he thought there had been an improvement; but, a week ago, he heard of something which had made him very miserable. He didn't dare to tell Mr. Chowdler; and though he had been within an ace, more than once, of asking the headmaster for advice, he had never quite made up his mind to do so. It was impossible to get the Prefects to act together, because a Prefect was himself involved, and the others wouldn't give him away. He had spent sleepless nights worrying over the business; but now he felt that he must make a clean breast of the whole matter. He wanted to do his duty; but he funked – there was no other word for it – the deadly unpopularity which was certain to be the result.

Mr. Flaggon first talked the boy into a calmer mood and then showed him, quietly and sympathetically, what his duty was. He must remove the seal of confidence and endure the unpopularity. The moral welfare of countless boys, present and to come, was at stake. And so, before he left the study, Dennison had braced himself to the most difficult act of courage that a boy can be called on to perform – namely, to defy a traditional code of honour and to face social ostracism.

An inquiry into Mr. Chowdler's house was necessarily a much more difficult business than an inquiry into Mr. Chase's. It was obviously impossible for the headmaster to take Mr. Chowdler into his confidence; so boys had to be sent for separately and interviewed in his own study. There was much coming and going, much leakage of knowledge and consequent reticence or denial. Mr. Flaggon felt that he had never sifted things quite to the bottom. But Dennison stuck to his guns; and, in the end, two boys, one of whom was a Prefect, were expelled at once, and four others were told that they must leave at the end of the term.

In the Prefect, Mr. Flaggon had long ago recognised one of the three youths who had impressed him so unfavourably on his first visit to Chiltern. In spite of the clearest evidence, this boy persisted in asserting his innocence, and on hearing his sentence he attempted a piece of insolent bluff.

'I shall appeal to Mr. Chowdler,' he said, 'and if he keeps me, I shall stay.'

Mr. Flaggon made no reply, but stepped quickly to the telephone. 'Number 92 A . . . Is the police inspector in? . . . No? Will he be in at six o'clock this evening? . . . Thanks. I may have to give somebody into custody . . . No thanks, there's no immediate hurry . . . if I want him then, I'll ring him up.'

And before he had readjusted the receiver, the boy, with a white face, blurted out, 'All right, sir, don't do that. I'll go at once.' And he left the study with his tail between his legs.

And on the following morning the school was summoned into the Great Hall at the end of first lesson and heard some words which nobody ever forgot. Anybody but Mr. Chowdler would have been overwhelmed by the sudden discovery of his own blindness; for in the two boys who had to leave so abruptly and for such hideous offences, he had always seen the true Chiltern type, the best product of the Lanchester tradition. But Mr. Chowdler was not an ordinary man. For a short time indeed he did feel as if the solid ground were crumbling again under his feet; but within a few days he had persuaded himself: first, that if there *had* been mischief in his house it was because 'the man Flaggon' had taken the control of it out of the proper hands; secondly, that boys had been bullied into confessing to crimes that they had never committed; and, thirdly, that there had been a great deal of hysteria and exaggeration about the whole business.

On this occasion, however, Mr. Chowdler found but few disciples. Mr. Flaggon's prompt and fearless handling of the affair, the words which he had spoken to the school, his genuine hatred of the evil thing and, with it all, his buoyant faith in the ultimate triumph of good influences, had made a deep impression on the masters. They realised that, in spite of youth and inexperience, the new headmaster was a man; and not a few of them felt that they had themselves been culpably blind.

'It's no good,' said one of the younger men, who taught a low form in the school, 'it's no good saying that we didn't see and couldn't be expected to see. We *ought* to have seen; the evidence was all around us. Why, there are three kids in my form – new last term – who are different men since this came out; different in their work and their manner and everything. It's like people waking up from a nightmare.'

'And there's one in my form,' said Mr. Rankin, 'who goes about looking as if he were going to be hanged. I guess he's got something pretty heavy on his conscience, and he's mortally afraid of being swept into the net.'

But there was one point on which opinion was not so unanimous. What would be the effect on the reputation of the school of all these drastic expulsions? Would not intending parents take fright? With numbers already down, was this root-and-branch method altogether wise – and was it really necessary?

Mr. Plummer shared these doubts; and he expressed them to Mr. Bent as they stood, one bleak afternoon in March, on the Sow's Back, looking over a grey and cheerless landscape.

'Of course,' he said, 'I recognise that Flaggon has come out of all this extraordinarily well, and has taught us all a great deal. Nothing, I'm sure, could have been more impressive than the way he spoke to the school, and I shall remember it as long as I live. But, I must say, I don't quite like this relentless pruning. Five boys on the spot, and ten more at the end of the term! It looks as if we were forgetting that it's our duty to save as well as to punish.'

'I know,' said Mr. Bent; 'the parable of the lost sheep. But that parable, my dear Plummer, was never meant for schoolmasters; *we* need to be reminded of our duty to the ninety-and-nine – we're always ready enough to play the rôle of good shepherd. Besides, you know the sequel.'

'What sequel?' asked Mr. Plummer.

'Don't you know,' replied Mr. Bent, 'that a month afterwards the lost sheep, having acquired a taste for adventure, trotted off into the wilderness again, taking with him this time the rest of the flock, twenty-five per cent of whom got eaten by wolves and never were heard of more? No, my dear Plummer, it's too risky.'

'But one *must* take risks,' insisted Mr. Plummer, 'if one is to do anything that is worth doing: and to refuse to take risks when there's a chance of saving anybody seems to me sheer cowardice.'

'Ah yes,' said Mr. Bent, 'true enough, if the risk were *our* risk – a danger to you and me. But it isn't. The danger is to the other boys – the boys who are here and the boys who are coming. If you want to make a public school a reformatory, you ought to be honest with the parents; you ought to say to them frankly, "I am keeping such and such boys, whom I know to be dangerous, because I think that the companionship of *your* son may possibly do them good." What d'you suppose that parents would say to that? What d'you imagine any of *our* married colleagues would say, if you proposed to plant a reformatory lad in the middle of their young families, because you felt sure it would be good for *him* and you weren't going to be scared by the risks? Answer me that!'

'There are reformatories and reformatories,' replied Mr. Plummer sententiously. 'Anyhow,' he added, as the dust-laden wind swept down the road, 'the prospect is gloomy – and I shouldn't wonder if we had some snow.'

Chapter 14

THE DAY OF DECISION

ONE evening, a week after this conversation, Mr. Bent received a summons to see the headmaster in his study after dinner; so, putting on his great-coat, for the wind was still blowing keenly from the north east, he repaired to the Prætorium. Mr. Flaggon was seated at his table, writing letters, but he waved his guest into an armchair and wheeled his own chair round to face the fire.

'I have to make arrangements for next term,' he began, with an abruptness that was characteristic. 'I am assuming that I shall be here and that Chowdler will have gone. In that case I want you to take his house.'

Mr. Bent was not altogether unprepared for this offer, though he had never allowed his thoughts to dwell much on the subject. He paused for a few moments before replying:

'It won't be a bed of roses – at least at first; but a year ago I should not have hesitated for a moment. To-day I know my limitations better, and I am not sure whether I have the necessary qualities.'

Mr. Flaggon eyed him keenly for a moment, and then said:

'I think you are more fitted for the post than anyone else here – if you will follow your better nature.'

'Then I will do my best,' said Mr. Bent, 'and trust that my better nature will pull me through.'

There was a pause before Mr. Flaggon began again, somewhat hesitatingly:

'I think, perhaps, that it would be better if this matter were kept private between us two – for the present at all events. I am thinking chiefly of your own position.'

'You mean,' said Mr. Bent, 'that, if certain things happen, I shall cut a better figure if I am found seated on the top of the fence than if I have come down definitely on the wrong side.'

Mr. Flaggon smiled. 'I suppose I meant something of the kind,' he said, 'though I didn't put it to myself quite in that way. The truth is that I am not at all sure about the future. I have every right to assume that the Council will support me against Chowdler; but, strictly between ourselves, they seem to be hesitating, and I have been approached lately with suggestions of a compromise. I can accept no compromise. It's not a question of my own dignity – though a public man has to consider that too: but if I am not to be headmaster *de facto* as well as *de jure*, I can serve no useful purpose by remaining here; and I shall go.'

'In that case,' said Mr. Bent, 'there is no need for secrecy; for, if you go, I shall go too.'

The headmaster coloured slightly. Ever since he had been at Chiltern, and especially in the last few weeks, he had felt his isolation and aloofness as no inconsiderable part of the burden. The sudden sense of fellowship sent a warm glow through his veins; but he repressed his emotion and replied gravely:

'I hope you won't do that; you mustn't do that. It is quite unnecessary, and it would damage the school.'

Mr. Bent got up from his chair, and, all unconsciously, began to pace about the room. His feelings were such that he could not express them adequately in a sitting posture.

'I'm not speaking on the spur of the moment,' he began. 'My mind was made up long before I came into this study and received your offer. For fifteen years I've lived in an atmosphere of bunkum and make-believe that have no relation to facts. That kind of thing is bound to make a man either a humbug or a cynic. It has very nearly made me a cynic; and, though it's very amusing to be a cynic, it isn't good for one's immortal soul. If one's to be a live man, one must have something definite to do –

something that one can believe in and work for. I *can* appreciate and work for your ideals – decency, order, and an education that – that is educational. I know that I shan't approve of all your methods – I'm Oxford, and much too critical for that – and you won't expect it of me. But I can *not* endure to sink back into unreality. I have enough to live on; not much but enough; and I can always get work – tutoring or anything. But I *will* not face another fifteen years of the off-theory and Chowdler's version of the Lanchester tradition. I say,' he added suddenly, 'I must apologise. In my excitement I've been forgetting my manners.'

The two men shook hands warmly at parting, and Mr. Flaggon was betrayed into something that very closely resembled a confidence.

'Of course,' he said, 'the long delay *is* rather trying.'

But the long delay was coming to an end, and the day of decision was fixed at last. Mr. Flaggon learned it from the Chairman of the Council; Mr. Chowdler and the masters were informed 'privately and confidentially' by Mr. Benison-Benison, and the boys heard of it from the masters' wives.

On the morning of the fateful day, Mr. Flaggon looked down the long rows of bowed heads in chapel with peculiar feelings. He was something of a fatalist, believing, as he did, that there is special Providence in the fall of a sparrow, and that a man is false to his duty, however hazardous that duty may be, if he allows himself to dwell on the possibility of failure. But he could not help wondering, that morning, whether he would ever sit in his place again and feel that his life's work lay there before him, and that he had the power to do it. In the last few weeks Chiltern had become to him something much more concrete than it had been before, something that stirred his affections and appealed to his sympathy. While searching in dark places for the roots of the parasite that was strangling the life of the place, he had discovered the germs of much that was healthy and even noble – individual heroisms, boys ready, at a moment's call, to do a man's work, knees which in the face of fierce temptation had never bowed to Baal; and with all its capacity for evil, he had realised the immense possibilities for good in schoolboy nature. He was conscious, too, of a change of attitude on the part of his staff. Rather shyly, rather awkwardly, many especially the younger men, had made it clear to him by voice and manner and gesture that they were with him. There was an irony in the fate which might give him the summons to quit at the very moment when he had secured a firm grip of the school and proved his right to rule. *Might* give? Very probably *would* give; for, in his heart of hearts, he had no great faith in the Council that was to pronounce judgment.

And, a few hours later, the councillors were assembling at Grandborough to decide between the headmaster and his rebellious lieutenant. Most of them had come with their minds more than half made up. That Mr. Chowdler's conduct had exceeded the courtesies of debate there could be no doubt; and, under ordinary circumstances, they would have been shy of interfering between a headmaster and one of his assistants. But the circumstances were not ordinary; and the men who were called upon to judge them were much influenced by the opinion, commonly expressed in Society (with a capital S), that the new headmaster was a failure and was letting the school down rapidly. They gathered, too, from Mr. Benison-Benison that this was also the opinion of the masters. And, again, they had been much alarmed by the recent troubles. Rumour had put the number of expulsions at 150; and though the councillors were now in possession of the correct figures, the impression remained that Chiltern, which had once seemed to be founded on a rock, was crumbling away before their very eyes.

'How do you intend to vote?' said Canon Braintree to Sir Arthur Tysoe, as they entered the assembly room at the 'Blue Boar,' which always served as Council-chamber.

'I shall vote,' said Sir Arthur, 'for any compromise that will save the assistant; he seems to be the better man. And you?'

'I shall vote against the headmaster,' replied the Canon; 'of course, it will mean his resignation, and may make us look a little foolish in the eyes of the world. Still, when one has made a mistake, the most courageous course is to undo it as soon as possible.'

When the councillors had got through a little preliminary chatting, they took their seats round the long mahogany table and the Chairman opened the proceedings.

'The business before us to-day,' he began, 'is to consider an appeal from the Rev. Henry Chowdler, assistant master at Chiltern, against a notice of dismissal, received from the headmaster on the 15th of February last, to take effect on and after the 7th of April proximo. In accordance with Schedule D, Clause 4 of the Statutes and Regulations, "any house-master, or other master, not being a dancing, writing or fencing master, who shall have completed fifteen years of continuous service on the staff" possesses this right. As Mr. Chowdler is one of the boarding-house masters at Chiltern and the headmaster has confirmed the notice of dismissal in writing to your Chairman, the appeal is in order. But you are no doubt aware that, under Schedule E, Clause 7, sub-section *b*, the Council is empowered to refuse cognisance of such an appeal, if it so thinks fit. This is a curious provision, and was inserted, I believe, at a time when Dr. Lanchester, who enjoyed the entire confidence of his Council, was having trouble with his staff. The first question therefore before us is, whether or no the Council will accept cognisance of the Rev. Henry Chowdler's appeal; and our decision in no way prejudices any subsequent action we may take when, and if, we proceed to consider the appeal on its own merits.'

The Chairman had rattled off his opening remarks with the volubility of a man who is accustomed to get through business quickly. He paused for breath and was about to add that, as the motion was presumably a merely formal one, he supposed there was no need for discussing it, when the Bishop intervened.

Somebody has said that no cause is irretrievably doomed until the Bishop of Grandborough has made it his own. Like all epigrams, this statement is only partially true; for the Bishop has championed many winning causes, good as well as bad. But his warmest admirers admit that, as a leader, he is more successful in putting heart into his followers than in winning over waverers.

'Technically,' he began, 'our Chairman is correct, and the motion does not prejudge the main issue; but, practically, it raises at once, and in an acute form, the question of confidence or no confidence in the headmaster. If we had merely to decide between Mr. Flaggon and Mr.

Chowdler, there could be no doubt as to what our decision would be; for every man in authority has a right to be supported against unruly subordinates. But we have not met here to judge between Mr. Flaggon and his subordinate. We are all aware that we have met to decide whether it is right or expedient that Mr. Flaggon should continue to be headmaster at all. That is an unfortunate position for us to be in, and if my advice had been taken last July, we should have avoided it. But we must take the situation as we find it and face it boldly. In my opinion Mr. Flaggon ought never to have been appointed and ought not now to be continued in his office; and I have with me convincing proofs to clinch my argument.'

Here the Bishop produced a large blue magazine, and held it up to show that there was no deception.

'In this magazine,' he continued, tapping the cover, 'there is an article by the Rev. Septimus Flaggon, entitled "Inspiration." When it was first brought to my notice, some weeks ago, I wrote at once to Mr. Flaggon to ask him whether he acknowledged the alleged authorship, and, if so, whether he was prepared to disavow certain passages in it, which I had marked with a blue pencil. Mr. Flaggon replied that the article in question had been written several years ago, but that, after re-reading it carefully, he saw nothing in it to retract. That being so, I propose to read you certain passages, from which you will be able to judge for yourselves whether the writer is a man who can safely be entrusted with the spiritual guidance of the young in a Church of England school.'

The Chairman here pointed out that Mr. Flaggon's theological opinions were irrelevant to the question at issue, namely, whether or no the Council should take cognisance of Mr. Chowdler's appeal. But the Bishop was not to be stopped.

'You will see the relevance,' he said, 'when I have finished.' And he proceeded to read out the incriminating passages. To about half the Council they seemed of the mildest and most harmless nature; and one of the members said bluntly:

'I see no reason why a headmaster should not hold these views, and preach them too if he likes. If we are going to begin heresy-hunting, I believe we shall make a grave mistake.'

The discussion, having once been launched on these troubled waters, was developed at great length and with ever-increasing acrimony. Inspiration was a subject which Mr. Benison-Benison had made his own and on which other members of the Council felt strongly. In vain the Chairman tried to recall the meeting to the real point at issue. He had to give way before the demands of human nature, and accept the inevitable. When at last the question was put, the voting went on strictly theological lines; with the result that the numbers for and against were exactly equal.

The Chairman hesitated. On the one hand he saw the unwisdom of practically installing Mr. Chowdler as permanent Mayor of the Palace at Chiltern. On the other hand, if Mr. Flaggon were going to empty the school, the financial situation would become difficult, and it might be better to do at once, what would probably have to be done later – namely, force his resignation.

The Bishop noted his hesitation, shrugged his shoulders impatiently, and whispered something to his neighbour. The words were inaudible, but the Chairman guessed their purport and his hesitation vanished.

'The question before us,' he said, 'being whether or no the Council will take cognisance of the appeal of the Rev. Henry Chowdler, and the ayes and noes being equally divided, I cast my vote in favour of the noes. As we have no further business to transact, the Council is adjourned to the 21st of June next, when I hope that the plans and estimates for the new sheds and pig-stye, to be erected on the boundary field, will be ready for approval.'

Chapter 15

AFTERMATH

MR. CHOWDLER took the blow standing. 'What else could you expect,' he said contemptuously, 'from such a Council! Like master, like man!' He did not even break down when his house gave him an ovation at prayers, such as might have greeted a conqueror. It was not so much a demonstration against the headmaster as a display of tribal loyalty to a fallen chief; and it had its touch of chivalry.

Mrs. Chowdler was completely bewildered. She could not understand how anybody, having to choose between Harry and that dreadful Mr. Flaggon, could fail to choose Harry. But she played up to her husband nobly. 'Of course,' she said, 'we never expected anything else; but Harry felt that it was his duty to give the Council a last chance of saving the school. They have rejected it, and that is the end of Chiltern.' Needless to say, nobody contradicted her, and she was the object of much silent sympathy.

Some people supposed, and many hoped, that when the verdict was given against him, Mr. Chowdler would leave at once or at least withdraw from active life; and the headmaster allowed it to be known in the Chowdler circle, through Mr. Chase, that if such a step were contemplated everything would be done to make it easy. But Mr. Chowdler preferred to die fighting. In deference to the entreaties of his friends, he did indeed absent himself from masters' meetings; but, otherwise, his presence was as much felt, his voice as often heard, as ever. No martyr has ever stood at the stake with a prouder or more defiant mien.

Now a martyrdom is always more of an unpleasant business for others than the victim; and one of the spectators who felt the unpleasantness most acutely was Mr. Bent. Mr. Bent repudiated the title of sportsman, but he had scruples and susceptibilities of his own. As unacknowledged heir to Mr. Chowdler's house he found his position a delicate one, and he hesitated to proclaim his right to the succession while Mr. Chowdler was so very much alive. It would have been comparatively easy to speak the word while the battle was still raging and the issue in doubt; but he had missed the psychological moment, and to speak it now, smacked too much of a mean triumph over a fallen foe. Therefore, when people wondered in his presence who would succeed to the house, he held his peace and felt a little like a boy who has committed an offence and fears to own up to it. The situation was particularly awkward, because it was high time that he should be making arrangements for moving in; and the holidays were short.

His friend Plummer put a finger, inadvertenly, one afternoon on the raw place and received a disagreeable shock.

'I wonder,' he said, 'who will get Chowdler's house. It's very tactful of Flaggon to keep it in abeyance; but he'll *have* to make the appointment soon – certainly before the end of term.'

'Perhaps it'll be *me*,' said Mr. Bent, colouring slightly.

'Impossible!' cried Mr. Plummer in a voice of genuine alarm. 'You're joking, I hope.'

'Why impossible, pray?' asked Mr. Bent, in tones of unusual chilliness.

'Why, because . . .' replied Mr. Plummer irritably, '. . . it's really very difficult to explain . . . but of all people you're the very last who ought to succeed Chowdler. Think what people would say!'

'*What* would they say?' asked Mr. Bent doggedly.

The task of enlightening an obtuse friend as to what people are saying of him is a delicate one; and Mr. Plummer couldn't help thinking that Bent was singularly and unexpectedly obtuse.

'Well, of course,' he began, 'it *has* been said by ill-natured people – when you became a Flaggonite, you know, and seemed to be seeing a good deal of him, that. . . . Well, in fact that you had an axe of your own to grind, and wanted—'

'The women, I suppose,' interrupted Mr. Bent.

'I expect so,' Mr. Plummer admitted.

Mr. Bent had always suspected that something of this kind would be said. But it is one thing to have disagreeable suspicions, and another to hear them confirmed. He looked pained, and said after a short pause:

'And do you believe it?'

'Of course not,' cried Mr. Plummer. 'Nobody who knows you would believe anything so ridiculous for a moment.'

'Then I don't see why I should mind,' said Mr. Bent.

'But, my dear fellow,' protested Mr. Plummer, 'you can surely see . . . and then there are the boys. Have you thought about them? Everybody knows – or at least thinks – that you have a special "down" on that house; and the boys—.'

'You mean they'll fight?' suggested Mr. Bent.

'Undoubtedly,' replied his friend.

'Good!' cried Mr. Bent. 'Excellent! Then there'll *be* a fight; that's all. It will be the making of me; and, by the Lord Harry, I'll smash 'em.'

There was only one other incident in the term that could be called at all sensational. At the last masters' meeting, about a week before the holidays, Mr. Flaggon distributed some printed papers, which were found to be a rough draft of the summer hours for Sunday, and a proposed new curriculum. 'I meant you to have these before,' he said, 'but I fear I have been too busy. I propose to discuss the whole question early next term.'

Mr. Beadle buried his head in his hands but said nothing; and almost everybody felt a slight shock of pained surprise. This was surely pushing the claims of the conqueror ungenerously far! They had accepted their new headmaster – had even begun to discover qualities in him which extorted admiration. But they expected that he, in his turn, would make concessions, come at least part of the way to meet them; whereas, to choose this particular moment for securing their tacit assent to disputed principles, seemed an unfair use of a delicate situation and peculiar circumstances. And it was inevitable that they should think so; for, as Mr. Bent observed, they could not understand that, what they were willing to accept as the end, was to Mr. Flaggon only the beginning.

The remaining days of the term lingered like an unwelcome guest who does not know how to take his leave. Everybody was nervously anxious to have got through without further shocks or excitement, to close a tragic chapter and plunge into the waters of oblivion before beginning a new page. For the strain of the past weeks had been almost intolerable.

And the end came at length, and in a gloom that made the last chapel seem like a funeral service. Dotted about among the congregation were the boys who were leaving under a cloud, and in his stall on the south wall of the nave sat Mr. Chowdler, red, unhappy, and defiant. Though he was convinced of the necessity, Mr. Flaggon could not but feel the pity of it all; indeed, for a moment, he experienced the sensations of a humane executioner in the presence of his victims. And worse was to come. For as he knelt for the last time in the school chapel, Mr. Chowdler was suddenly overpowered by his emotions, and his broad shoulders shook with the sobs that he was powerless to control. It was not remorse; it was not even regret for anything he had done. Something there was of the bitterness of defeat, and something of the grief of a sanguine man who has lost an only child. Mr. Chowdler had loved Chiltern with all the strength of a robust and unimaginative nature; and in a few short months he had seen his roots in the past and his heritage in the future destroyed, utterly and for ever. The holy places had been defiled and Jerusalem made a heap of stones.

The headmaster saw and understood; and he had to make an unusual effort before he was able to pronounce the blessing.

With the departure of Mr. Chowdler the Lanchester Tradition, according to one school of thought, received its death-blow. According to another, it was really disinterred and given a new lease of life; and a pamphlet containing some hitherto unpublished letters of the great man, which can be obtained at the school stationer's, lends some colour to this view.

What Mr. Flaggon made of Chiltern and how Mr. Bent fared with his house, may, possibly, be told hereafter. For the present, we will leave them to fight out their battles under the eyes of watchful colleagues and the shadow of Dr. Lanchester's statue in the great quadrangle.

THE END